SUPER POTATO

#7 SUPER POTATO AND THE GREENHOUSE OF EVIL

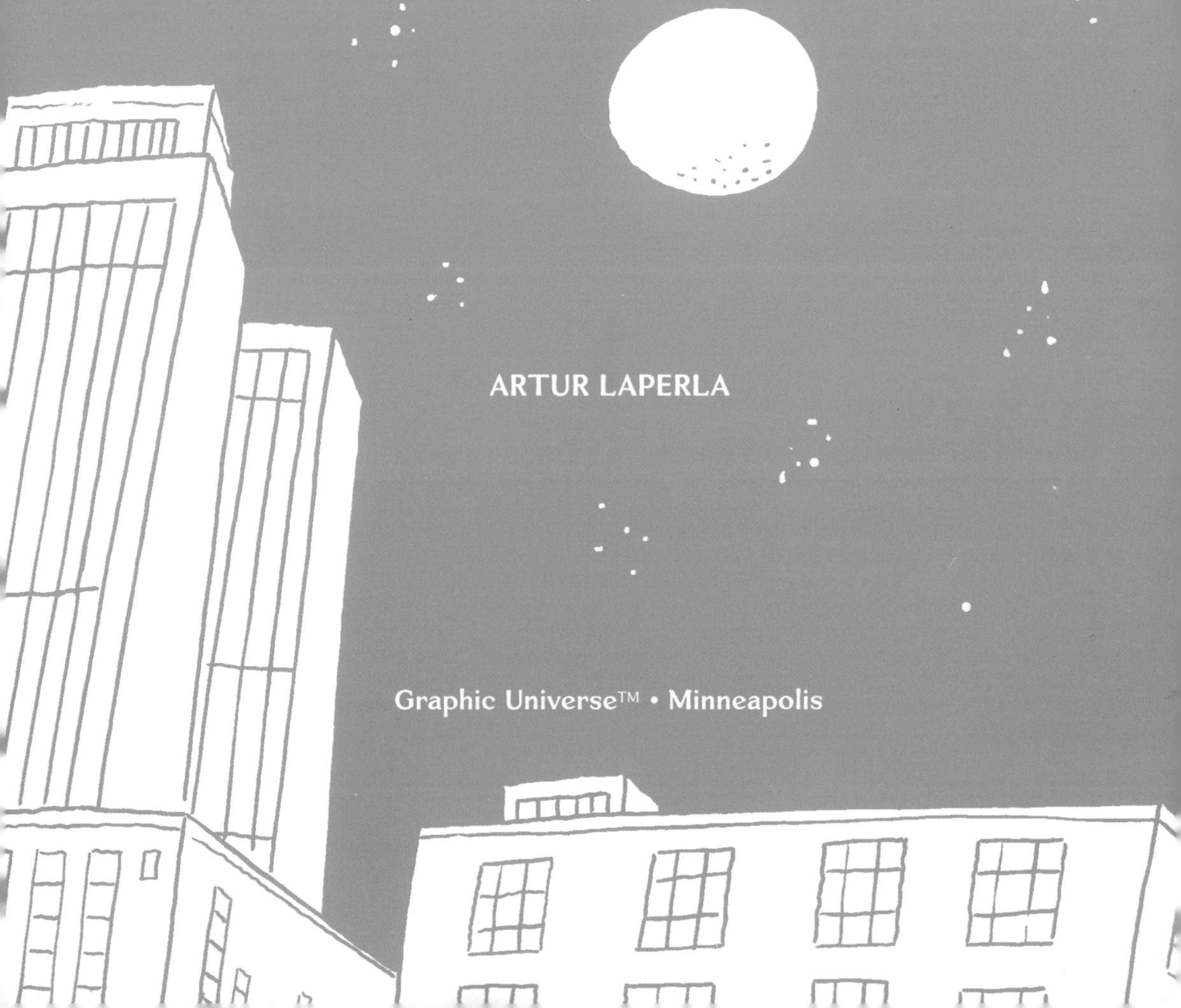

ARTUR LAPERLA

Graphic Universe™ • Minneapolis

Story and illustrations by Artur Laperla
Translation by Norwyn MacTíre

First American edition published in 2021 by Graphic Universe™

Copyright © 2017 by Artur Laperla and Bang. Ediciones.

Graphic Universe™ is a trademark of Lerner Publishing Group, Inc.

All US rights reserved. No part of this book may be reproduced, stored in a retrieval system, or transmitted in any form or by any means—electronic, mechanical, photocopying, recording, or otherwise—without the prior written permission of Lerner Publishing Group, Inc., except for the inclusion of brief quotations in an acknowledged review.

Graphic Universe™
An imprint of Lerner Publishing Group, Inc.
241 First Avenue North
Minneapolis, MN 55401 USA

For reading levels and more information, look up this title at www.lernerbooks.com.

Main body text set in CCWildWords. Typeface provided by Comicraft.

Library of Congress Cataloging-in-Publication Data

Names: Laperla (Artist), author, illustrator. | MacTíre, Norwyn, translator.
Title: Super Potato and the greenhouse of evil / Artur Laperla ; translation by Norwyn MacTíre.
Other titles: Super Patata (Series). English
Description: First American edition. | Minneapolis : Graphic Universe, 2021. | Series: Super Potato ; book 7 | Audience: Ages 7–11 | Audience: Grades 2–3 | Summary: "Super Potato's archenemy Doctor Malevolent has returned, and this time he has a plant-based plan to take over the world!" —Provided by publisher.
Identifiers: LCCN 2020046465 (print) | LCCN 2020046466 (ebook) | ISBN 9781728424576 (library binding) | ISBN 9781728431093 (paperback) | ISBN 9781728438832 (ebook)
Subjects: LCSH: Graphic novels. | CYAC: Graphic novels. | Superheroes—Fiction. | Potatoes—Fiction. | Humorous stories.
Classification: LCC PZ7.7.L367 Sp 2021 (print) | LCC PZ7.7.L367 (ebook) | DDC 741.5/973—dc23

LC record available at https://lccn.loc.gov/2020046465
LC ebook record available at https://lccn.loc.gov/2020046466

Manufactured in the United States of America
1-49326-49442-12/14/2020

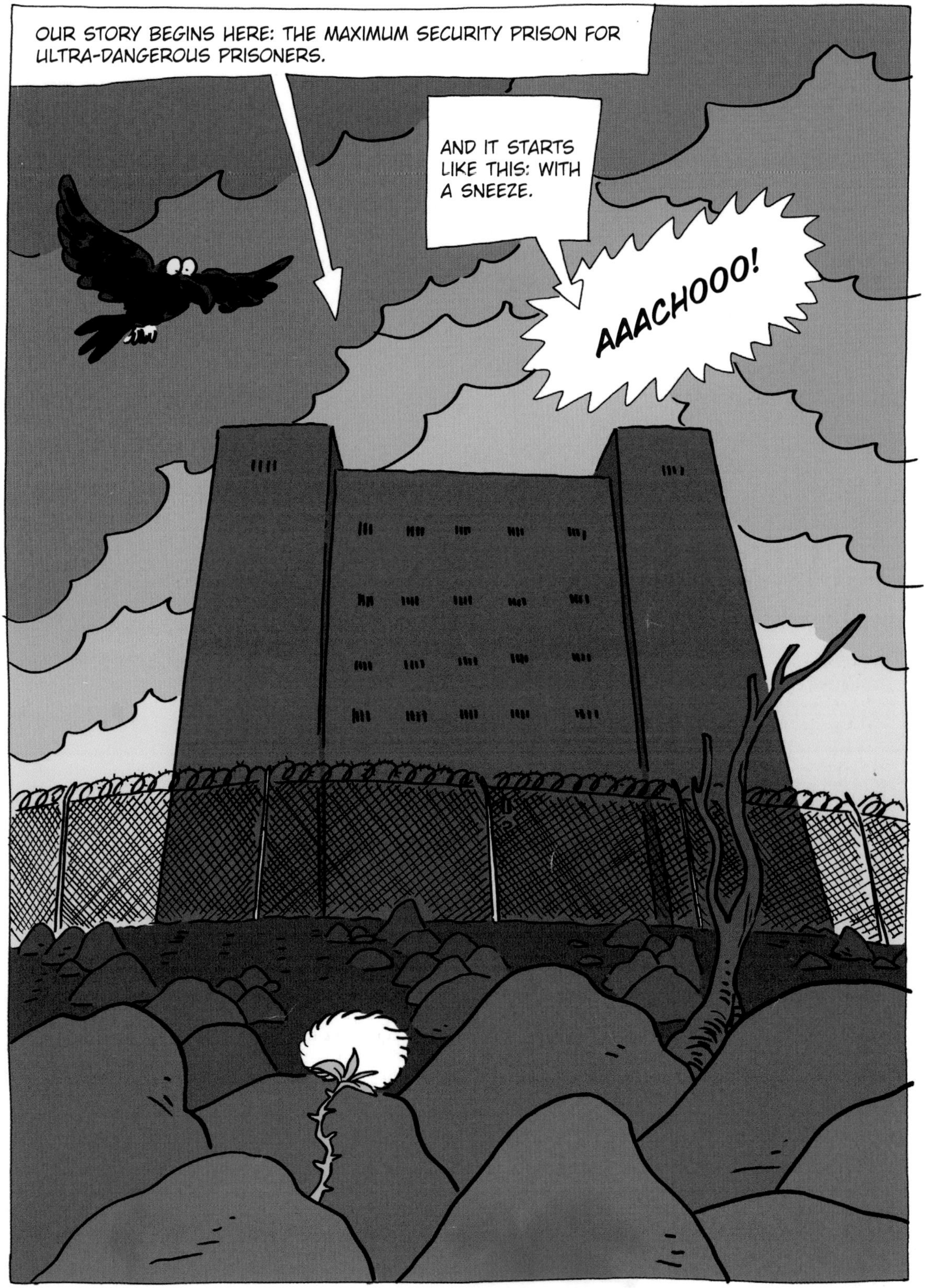
OUR STORY BEGINS HERE: THE MAXIMUM SECURITY PRISON FOR ULTRA-DANGEROUS PRISONERS.
AND IT STARTS LIKE THIS: WITH A SNEEZE.
AAACHOOO!

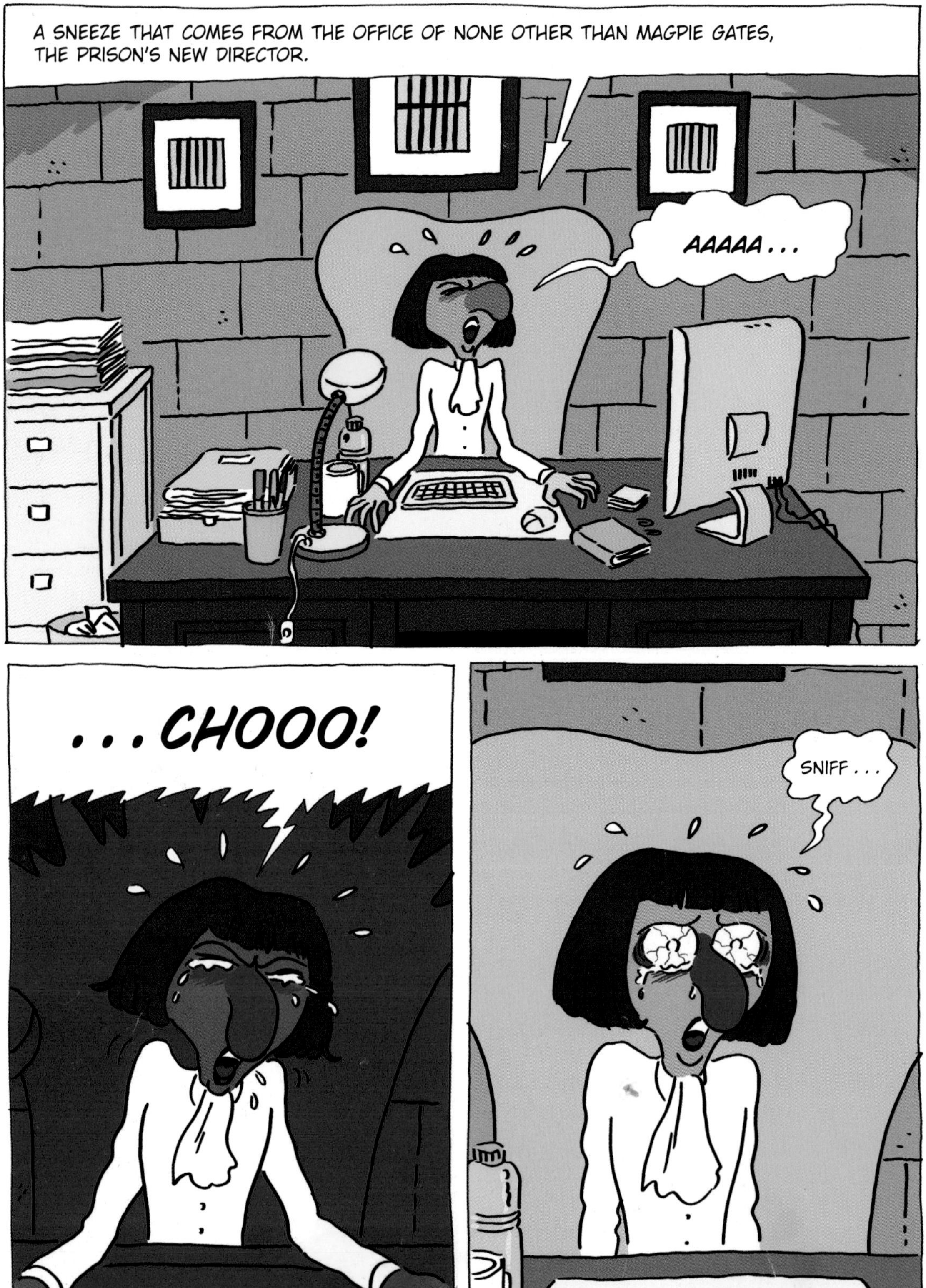
A SNEEZE THAT COMES FROM THE OFFICE OF NONE OTHER THAN MAGPIE GATES, THE PRISON'S NEW DIRECTOR.
AAAAA . . .
. . . CHOOO!
SNIFF . . .

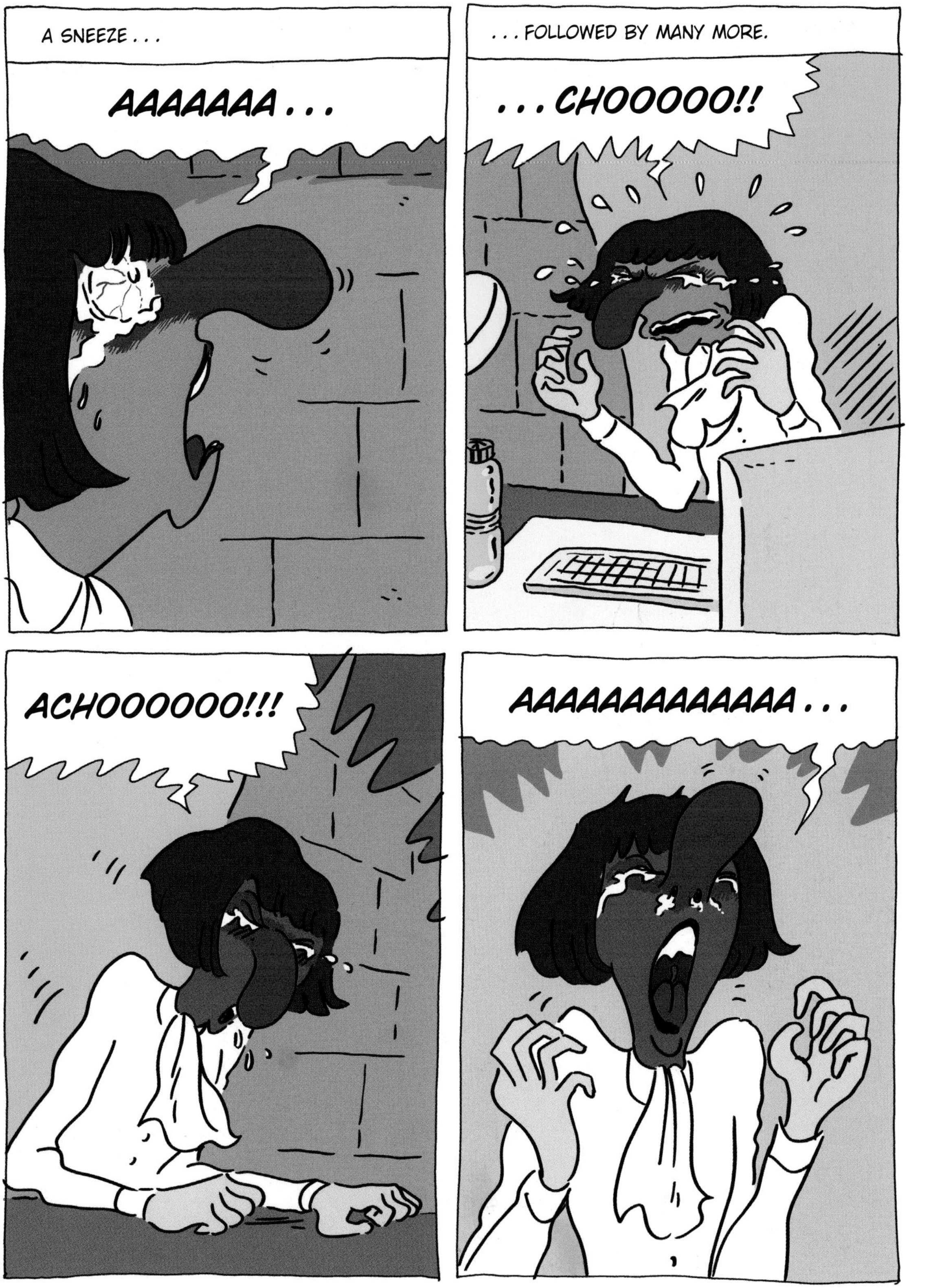
A SNEEZE . . .
AAAAAAA . . .
. . . FOLLOWED BY MANY MORE.
. . . CHOOOOO!!
ACHOOOOOOO!!!
AAAAAAAAAAAAA . . .

MEANWHILE . . . IN THE VERY SAME MAXIMUM SECURITY PRISON, OVER IN CELL 10509, DOCTOR MALEVOLENT IS PEACEFULLY SERVING HIS SENTENCE, DEDICATED TO HIS GREATEST PASSION: FLORICULTURE.

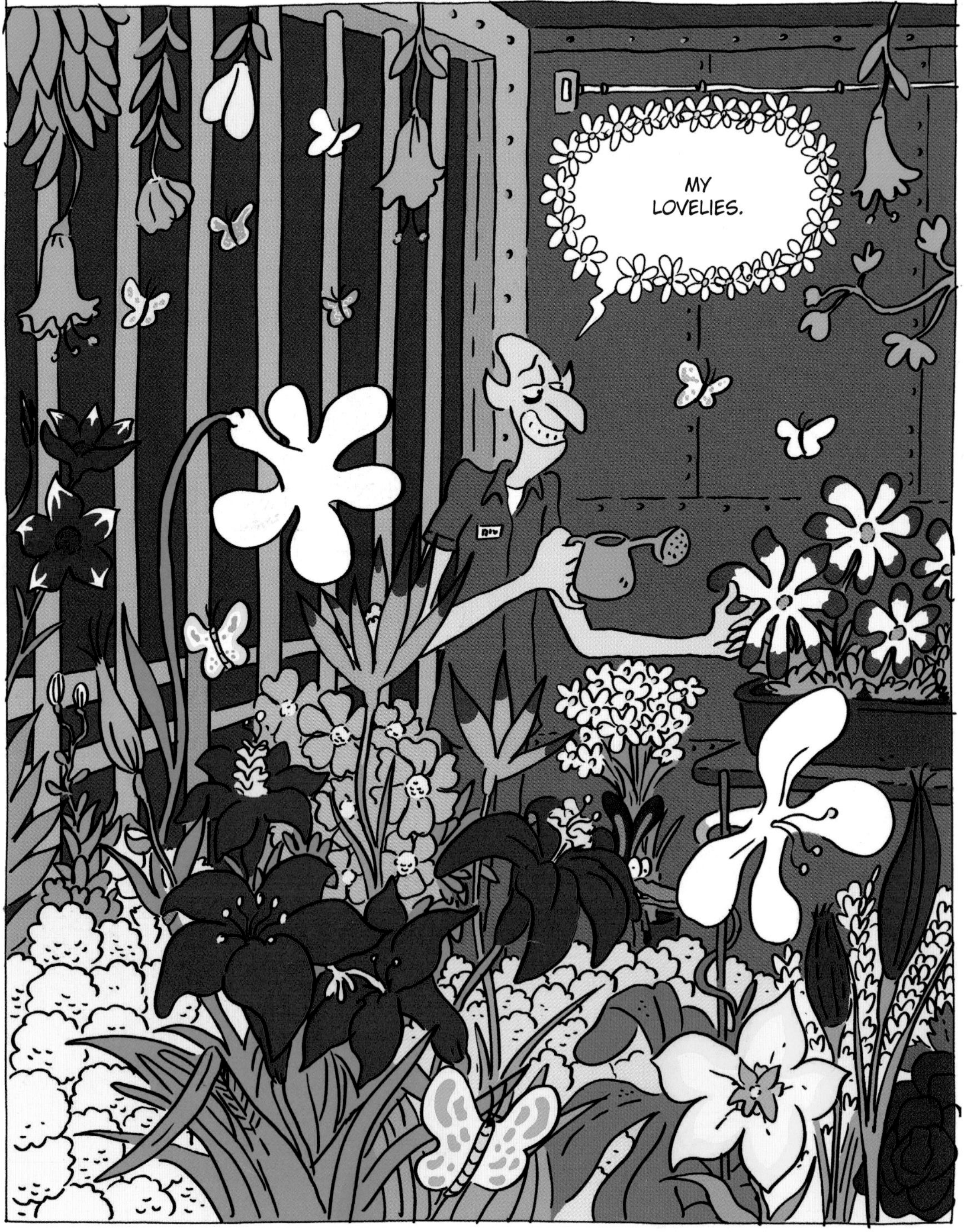
MY LOVELIES.

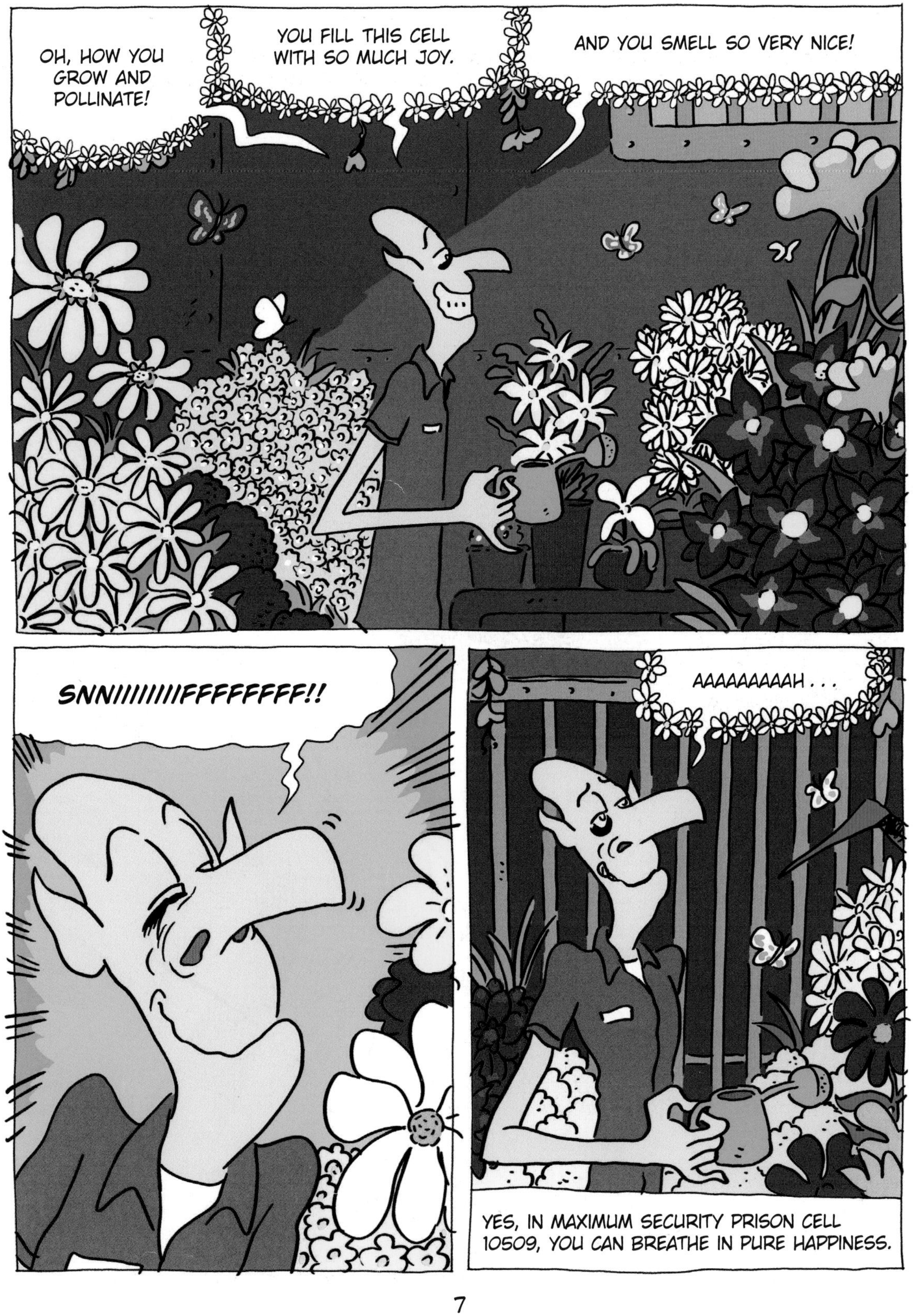
OH, HOW YOU GROW AND POLLINATE!
YOU FILL THIS CELL WITH SO MUCH JOY.
AND YOU SMELL SO VERY NICE!
SNNIIIIIIIIFFFFFFFF!!
AAAAAAAAAH . . .
YES, IN MAXIMUM SECURITY PRISON CELL 10509, YOU CAN BREATHE IN PURE HAPPINESS.

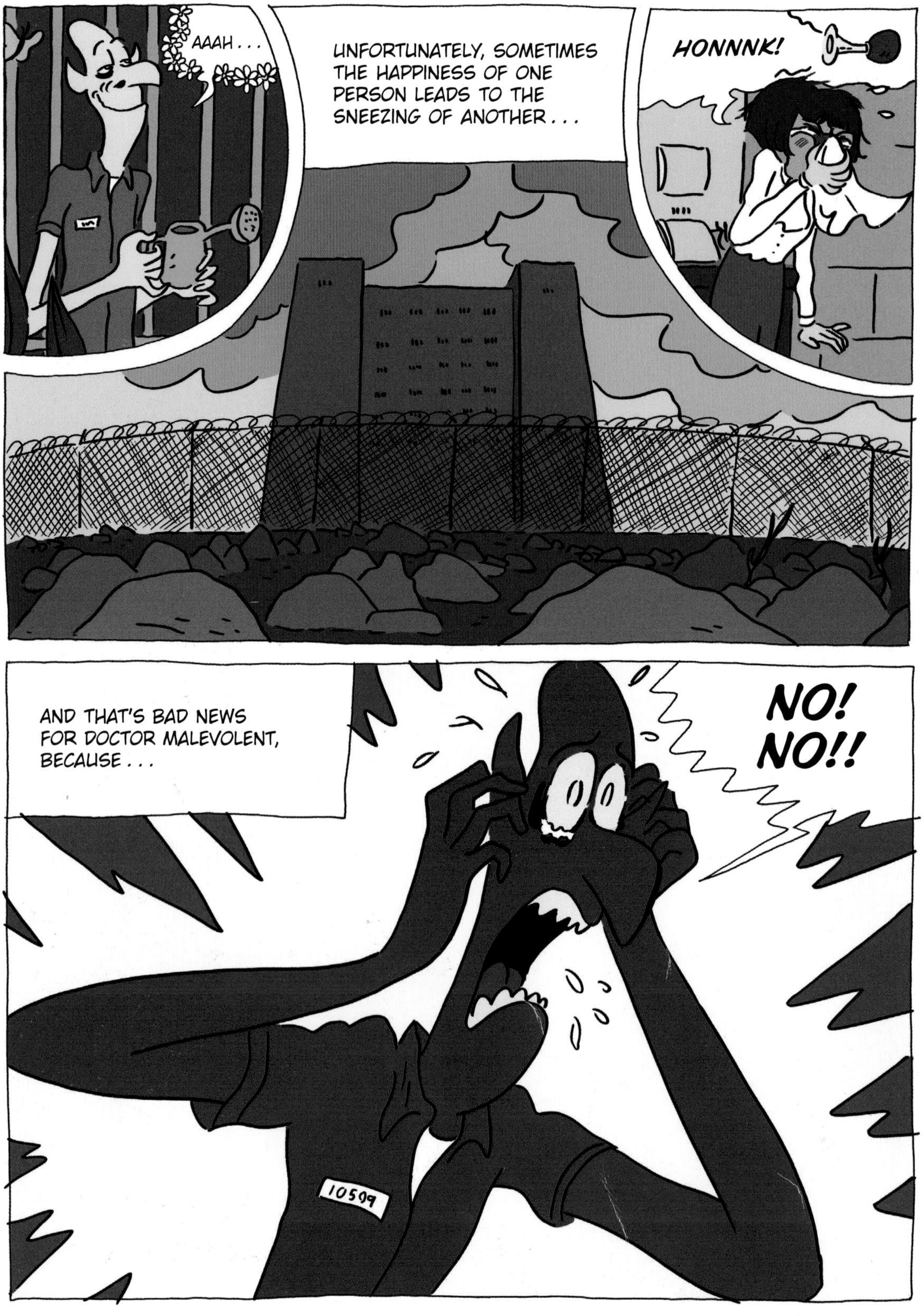
AAAH . . .
UNFORTUNATELY, SOMETIMES THE HAPPINESS OF ONE PERSON LEADS TO THE SNEEZING OF ANOTHER . . .
HONNNK!
AND THAT'S BAD NEWS FOR DOCTOR MALEVOLENT, BECAUSE . . .
NO! NO!!
10509

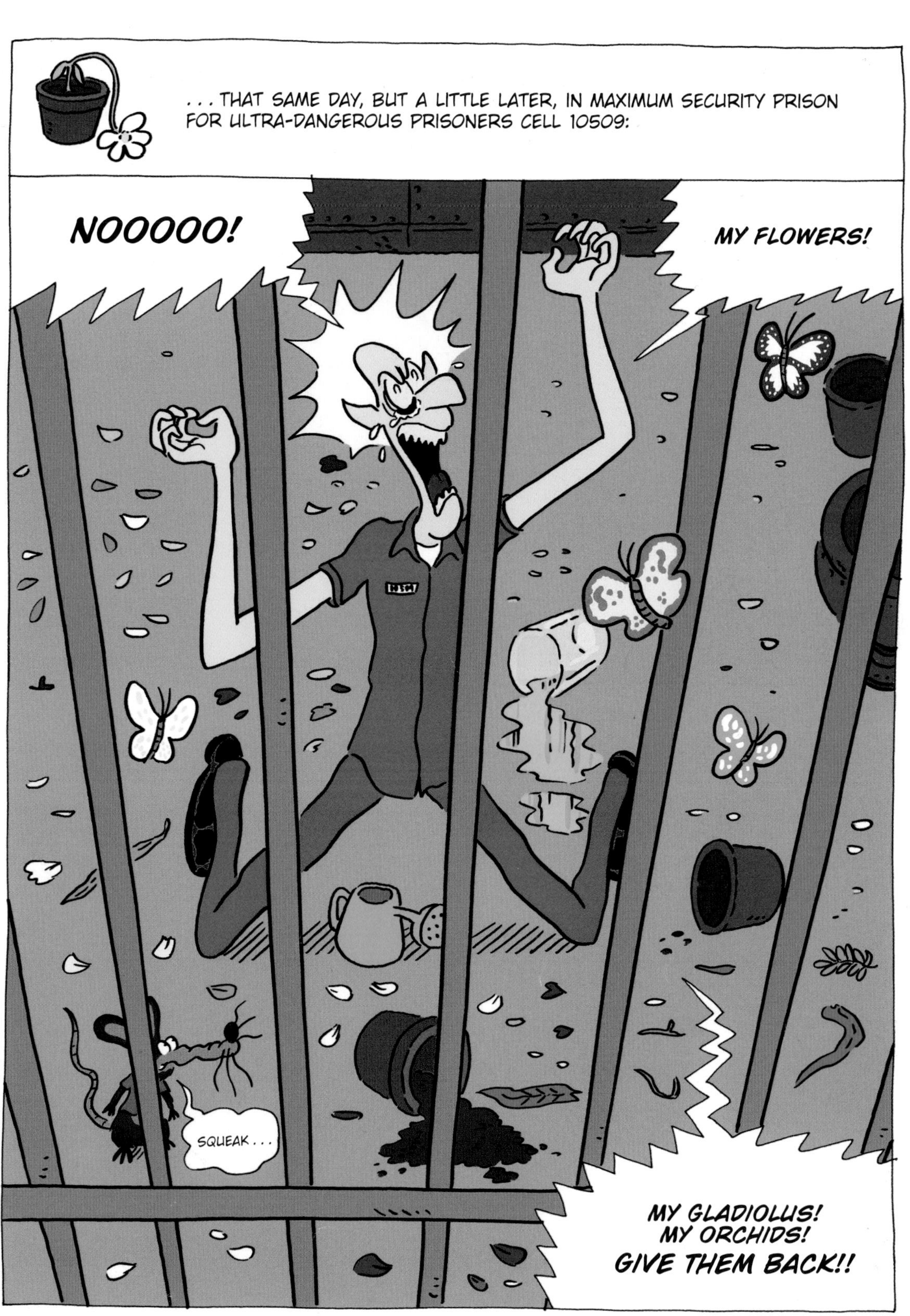
. . . THAT SAME DAY, BUT A LITTLE LATER, IN MAXIMUM SECURITY PRISON FOR ULTRA-DANGEROUS PRISONERS CELL 10509:
NOOOOO!
MY FLOWERS!
SQUEAK . . .
MY GLADIOLUS! MY ORCHIDS! GIVE THEM BACK!!

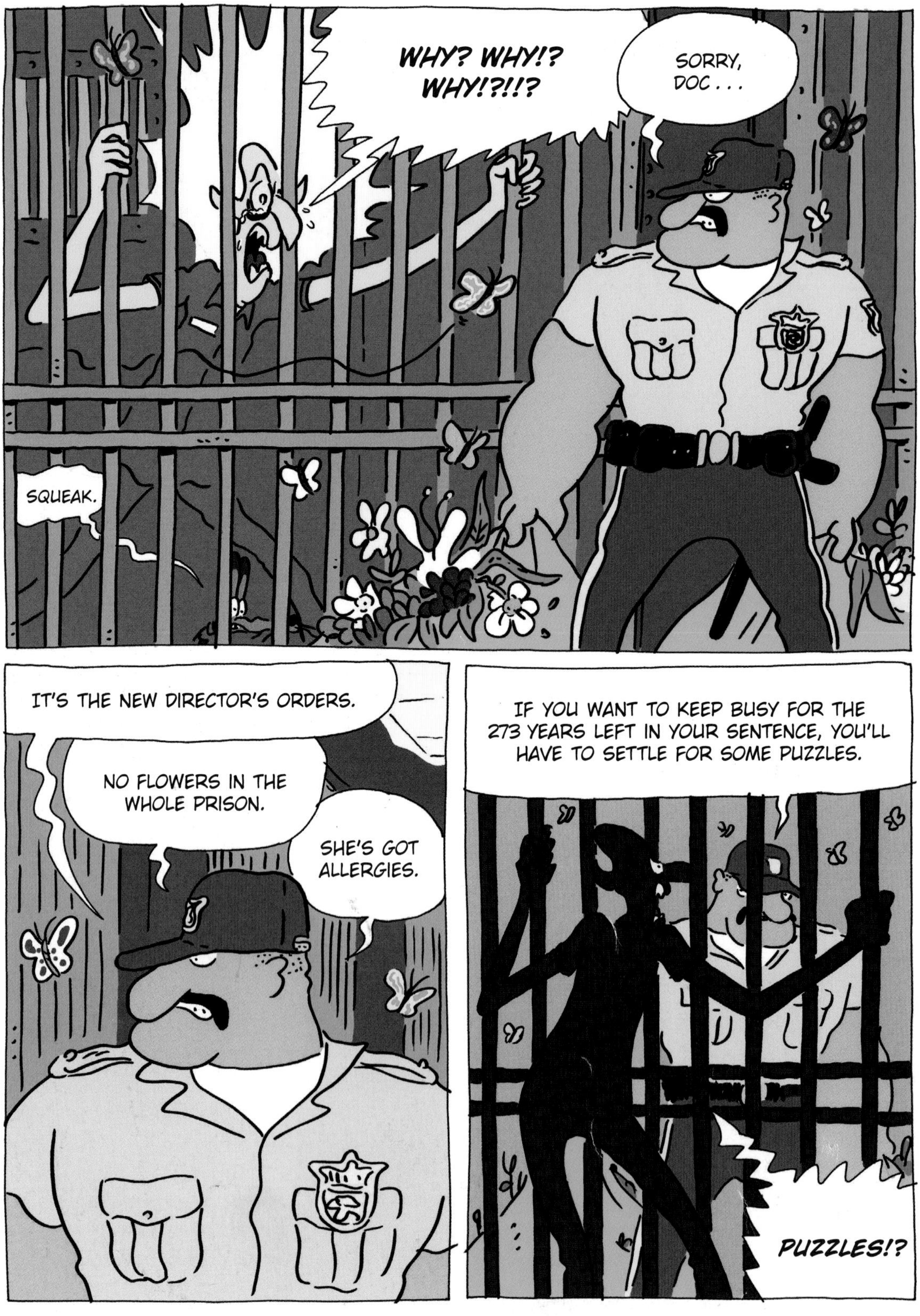
WHY? WHY!? WHY!?!!?
SORRY, DOC . . .
SQUEAK.
IT'S THE NEW DIRECTOR'S ORDERS.
NO FLOWERS IN THE WHOLE PRISON.
SHE'S GOT ALLERGIES.
IF YOU WANT TO KEEP BUSY FOR THE 273 YEARS LEFT IN YOUR SENTENCE, YOU'LL HAVE TO SETTLE FOR SOME PUZZLES.
PUZZLES!?

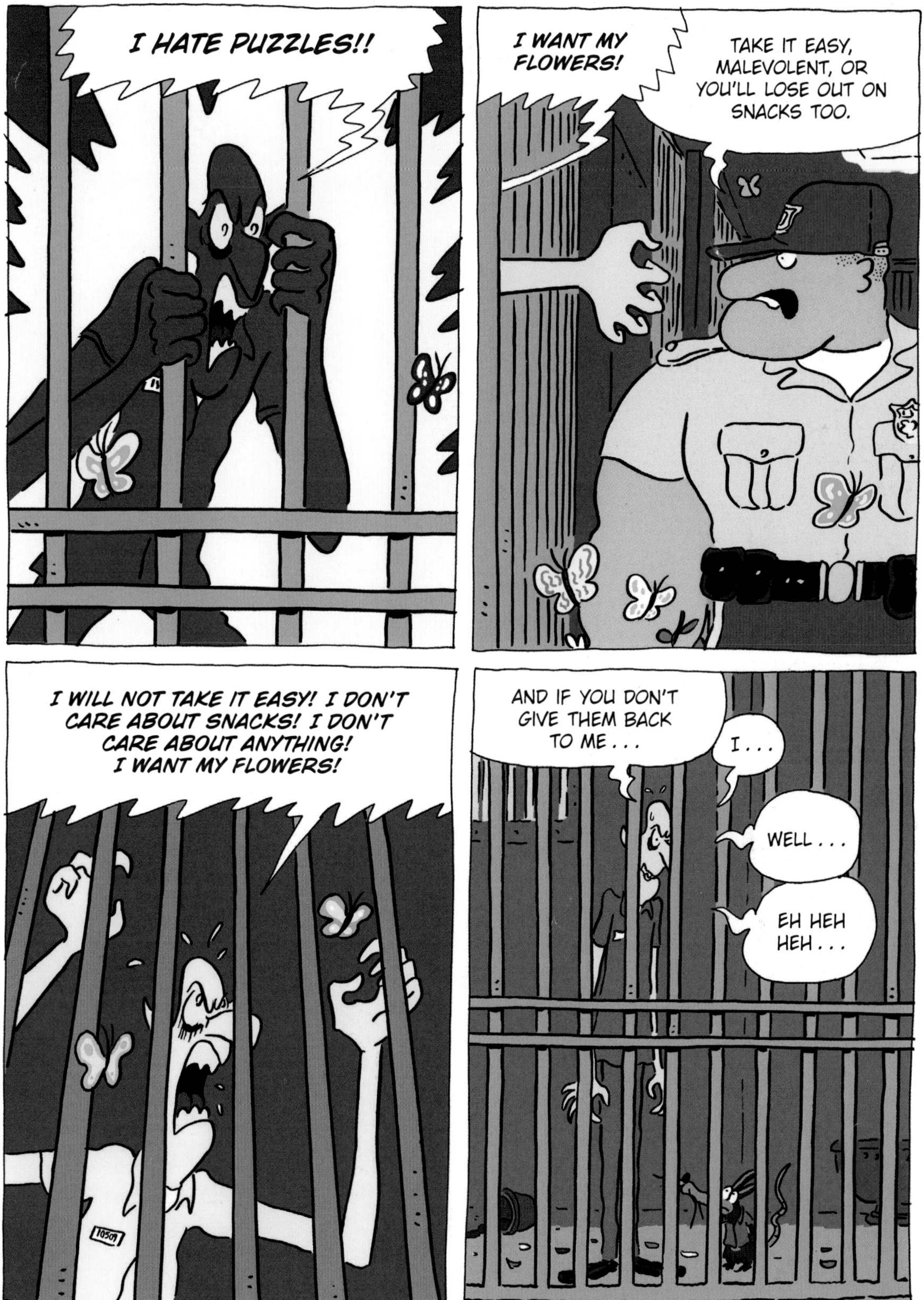
I HATE PUZZLES!!
I WANT MY FLOWERS!
TAKE IT EASY, MALEVOLENT, OR YOU'LL LOSE OUT ON SNACKS TOO.
I WILL NOT TAKE IT EASY! I DON'T CARE ABOUT SNACKS! I DON'T CARE ABOUT ANYTHING! I WANT MY FLOWERS!
AND IF YOU DON'T GIVE THEM BACK TO ME . . .
I . . .
WELL . . .
EH HEH HEH . . .

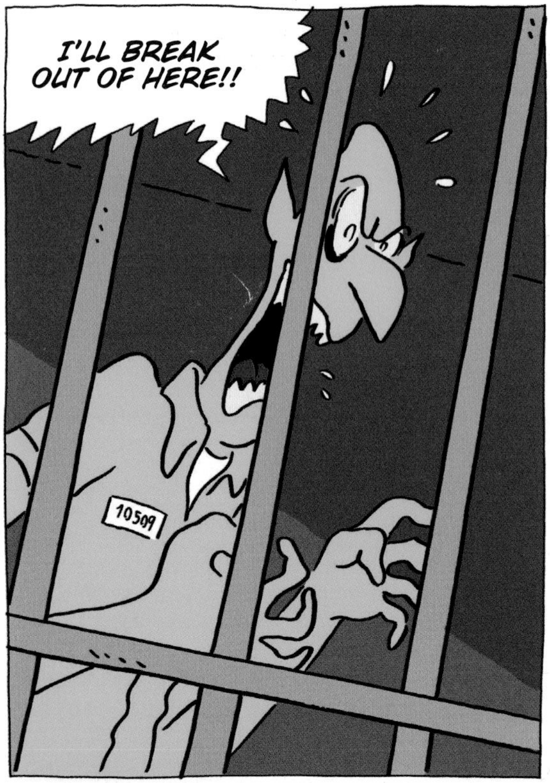
I'LL BREAK OUT OF HERE!!
10509

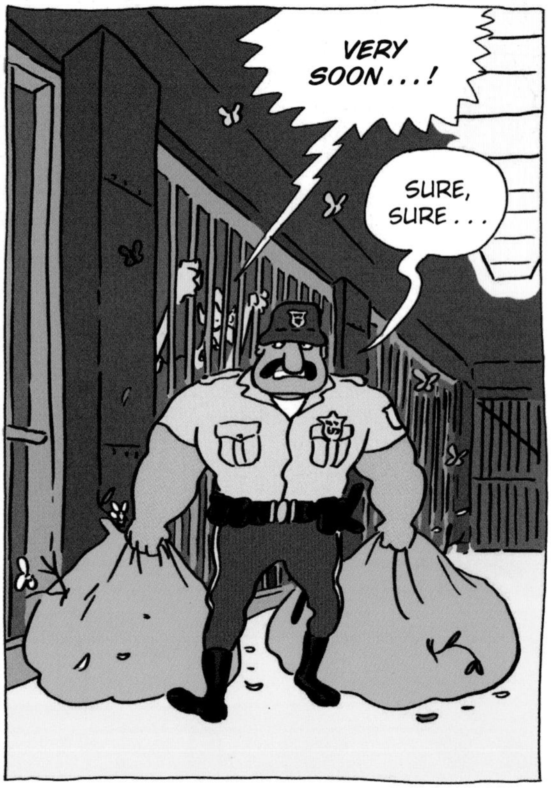
VERY SOON . . . !
SURE, SURE . . .

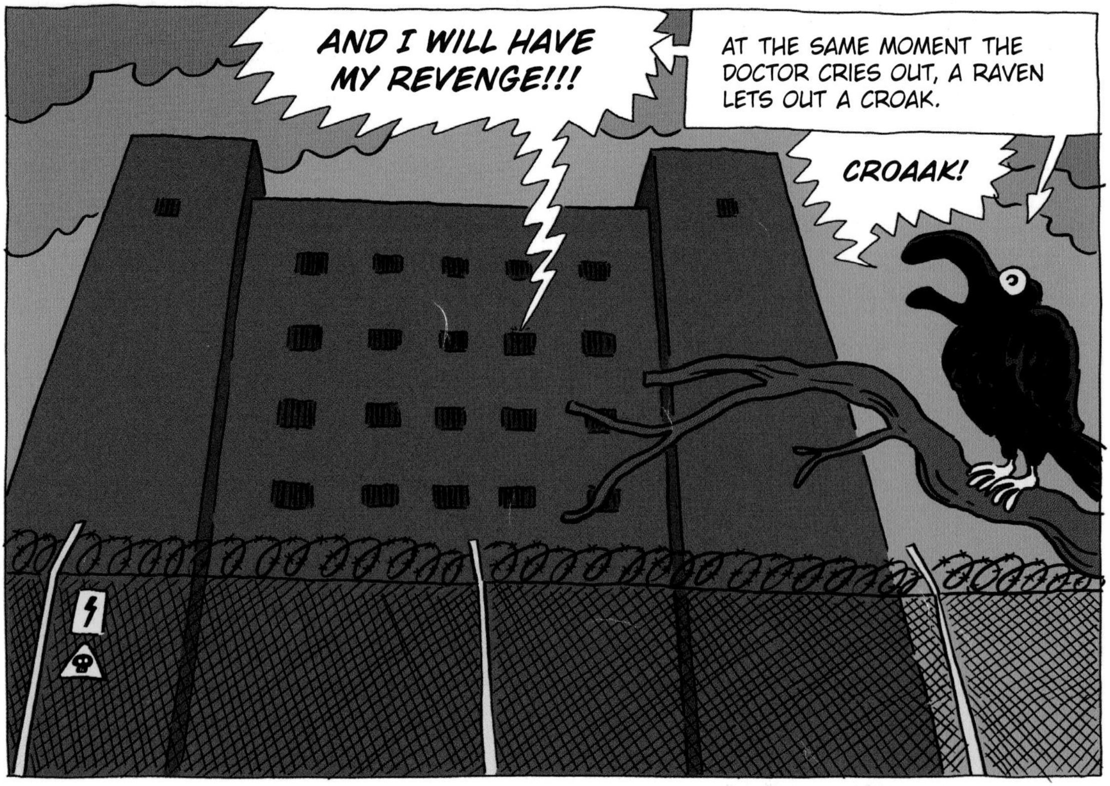
AND I WILL HAVE MY REVENGE!!!
AT THE SAME MOMENT THE DOCTOR CRIES OUT, A RAVEN LETS OUT A CROAK.
CROAAK!

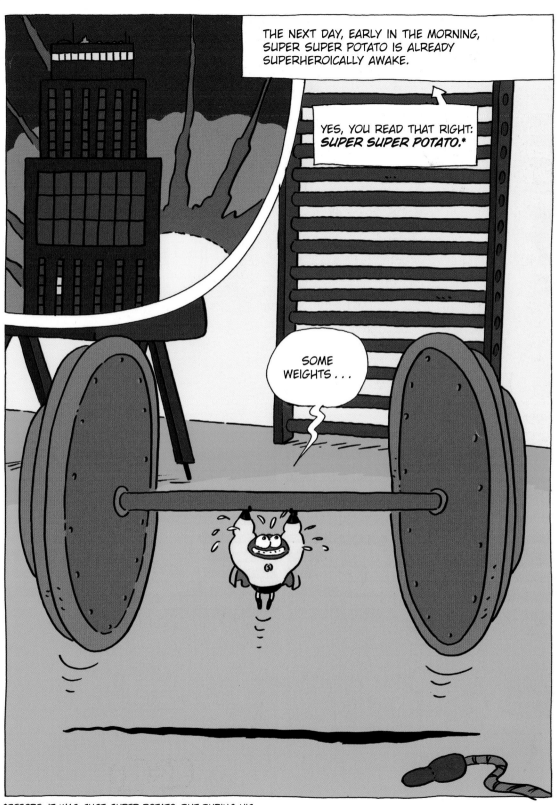

THE NEXT DAY, EARLY IN THE MORNING, SUPER SUPER POTATO IS ALREADY SUPERHEROICALLY AWAKE.

YES, YOU READ THAT RIGHT: *SUPER SUPER POTATO.**

SOME WEIGHTS . . .

*BEFORE, IT WAS JUST SUPER POTATO, BUT DURING HIS LAST ADVENTURE, HE PUT ON A LOT MORE MUSCLE.

13

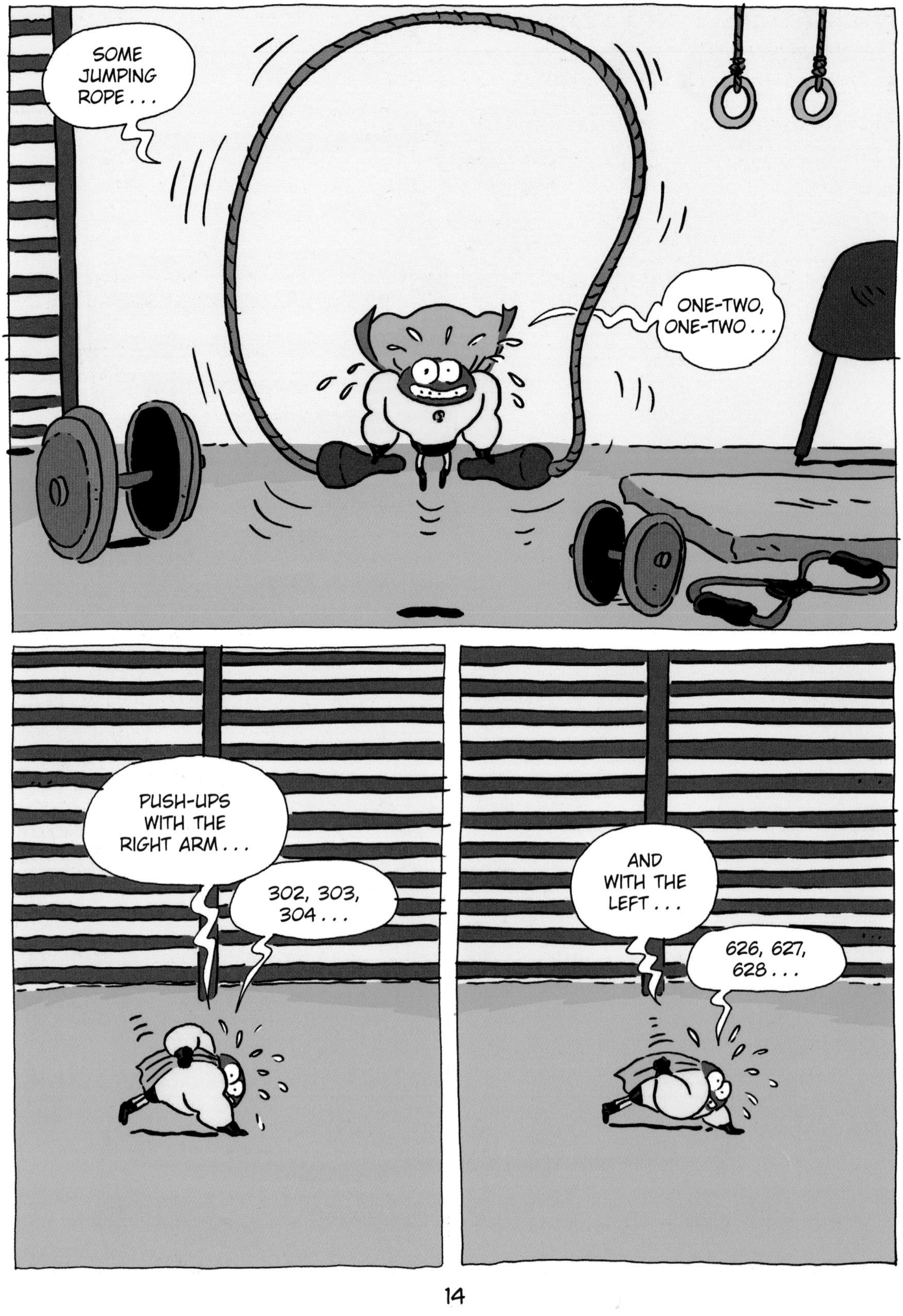
SOME JUMPING ROPE . . .
ONE-TWO, ONE-TWO . . .
PUSH-UPS WITH THE RIGHT ARM . . .
302, 303, 304 . . .
AND WITH THE LEFT . . .
626, 627, 628 . . .

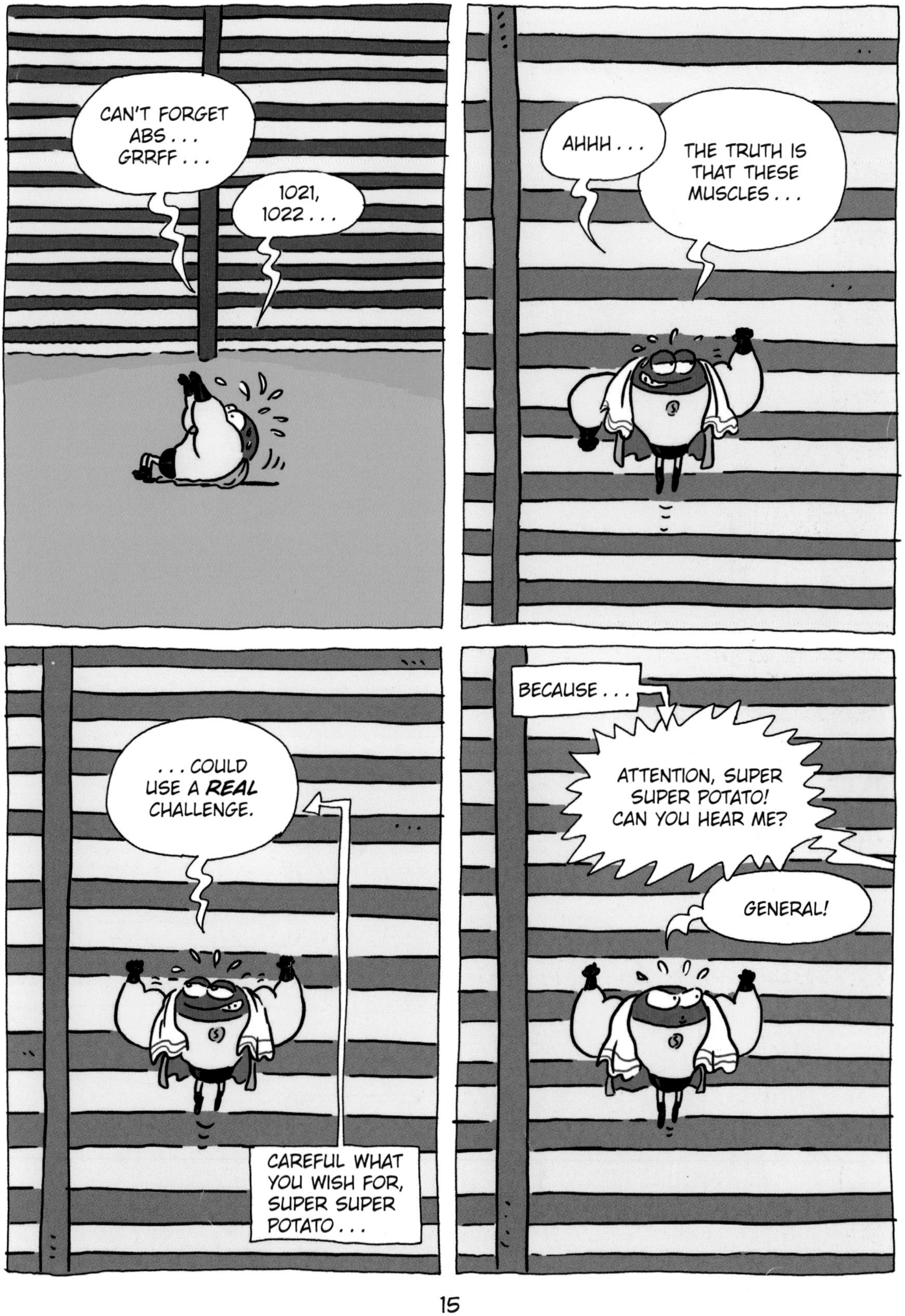
CAN'T FORGET ABS . . . GRRFF . . .
1021, 1022 . . .
AHHH . . .
THE TRUTH IS THAT THESE MUSCLES . . .
. . . COULD USE A ***REAL*** CHALLENGE.
CAREFUL WHAT YOU WISH FOR, SUPER SUPER POTATO . . .
BECAUSE . . .
ATTENTION, SUPER SUPER POTATO! CAN YOU HEAR ME?
GENERAL!

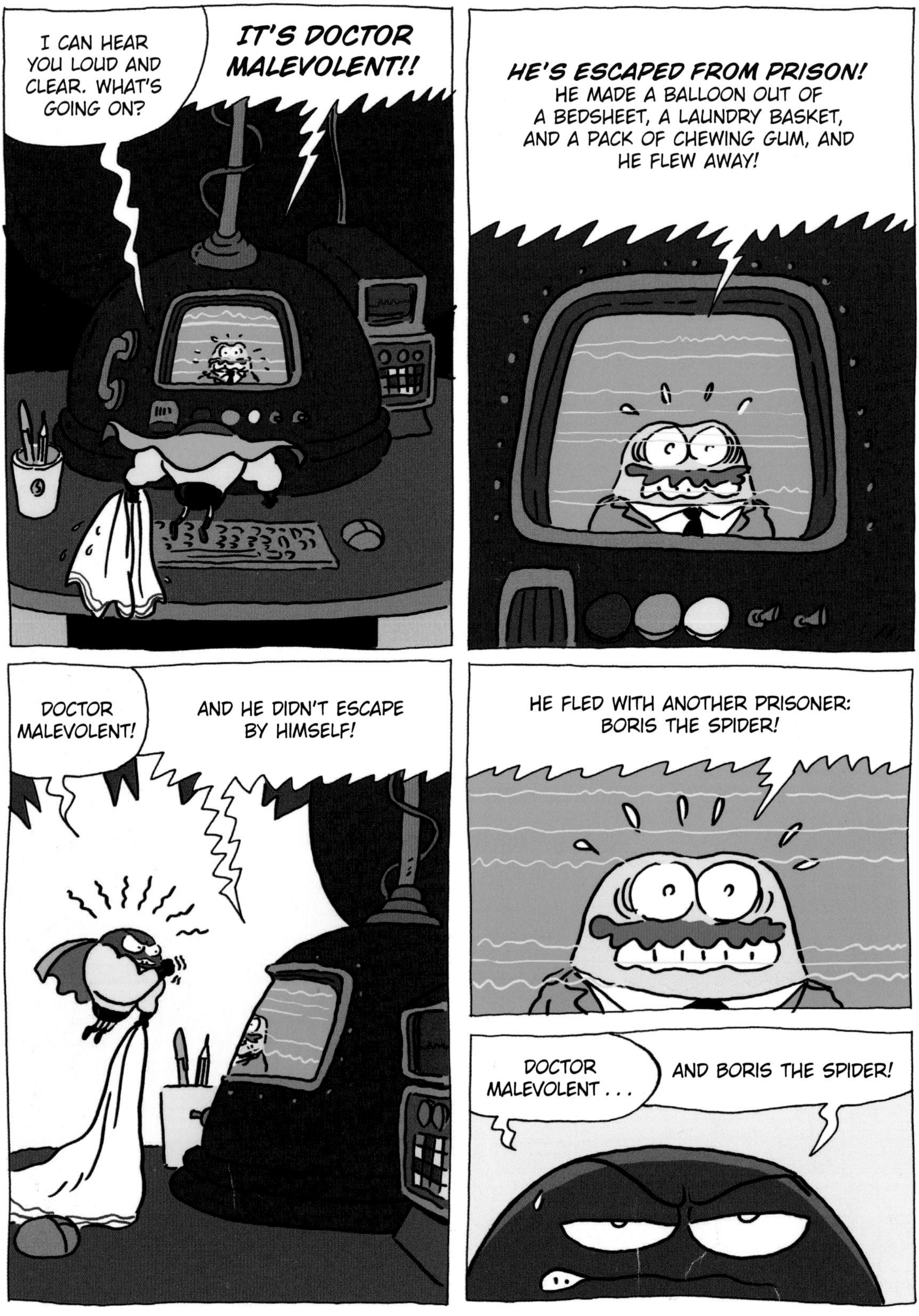
I CAN HEAR YOU LOUD AND CLEAR. WHAT'S GOING ON?
IT'S DOCTOR MALEVOLENT!!
HE'S ESCAPED FROM PRISON! HE MADE A BALLOON OUT OF A BEDSHEET, A LAUNDRY BASKET, AND A PACK OF CHEWING GUM, AND HE FLEW AWAY!
DOCTOR MALEVOLENT!
AND HE DIDN'T ESCAPE BY HIMSELF!
HE FLED WITH ANOTHER PRISONER: BORIS THE SPIDER!
DOCTOR MALEVOLENT . . .
AND BORIS THE SPIDER!

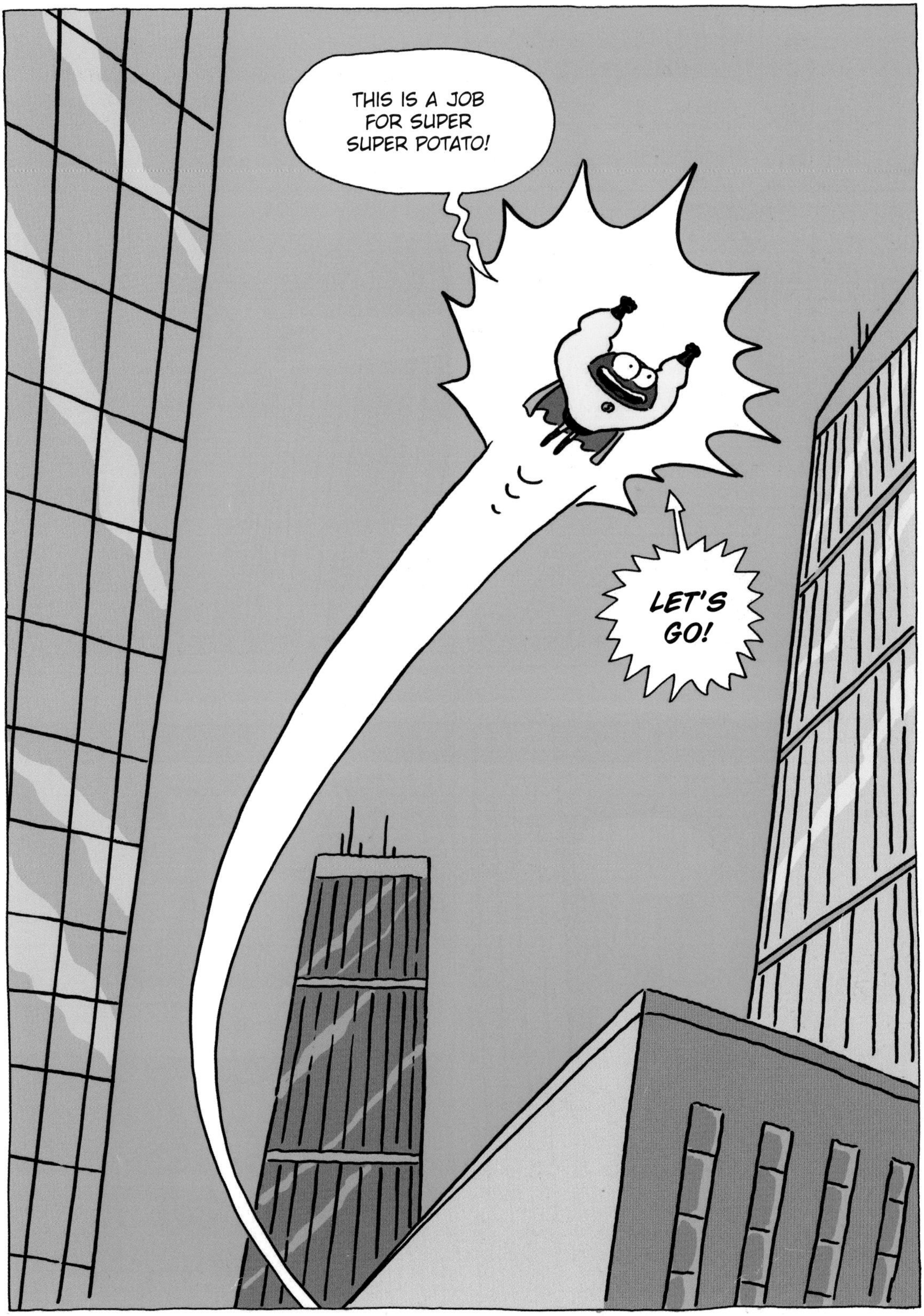
THIS IS A JOB FOR SUPER SUPER POTATO!
LET'S GO!

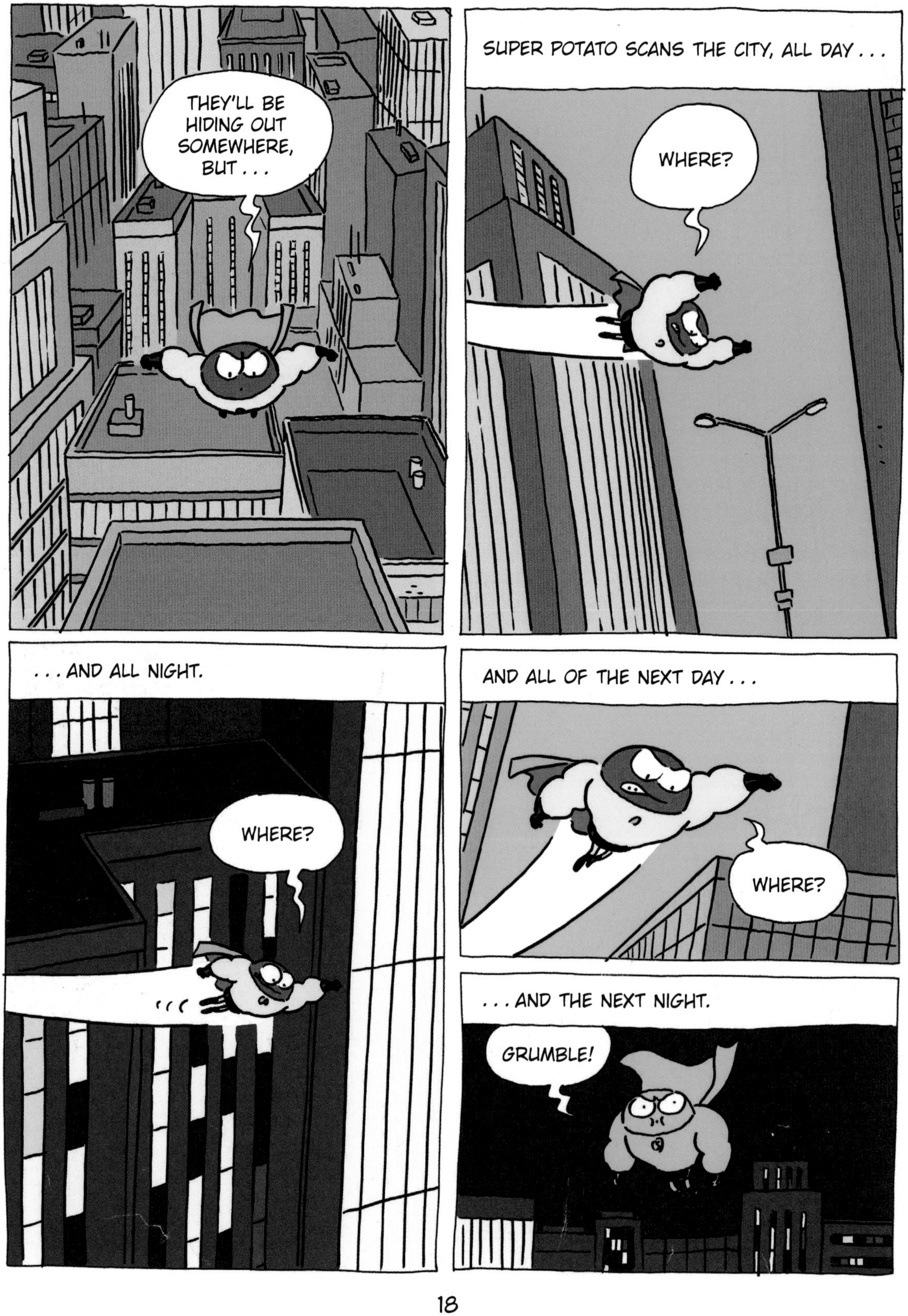
THEY'LL BE HIDING OUT SOMEWHERE, BUT . . .
SUPER POTATO SCANS THE CITY, ALL DAY . . .
WHERE?
. . . AND ALL NIGHT.
WHERE?
AND ALL OF THE NEXT DAY . . .
WHERE?
. . . AND THE NEXT NIGHT.
GRUMBLE!

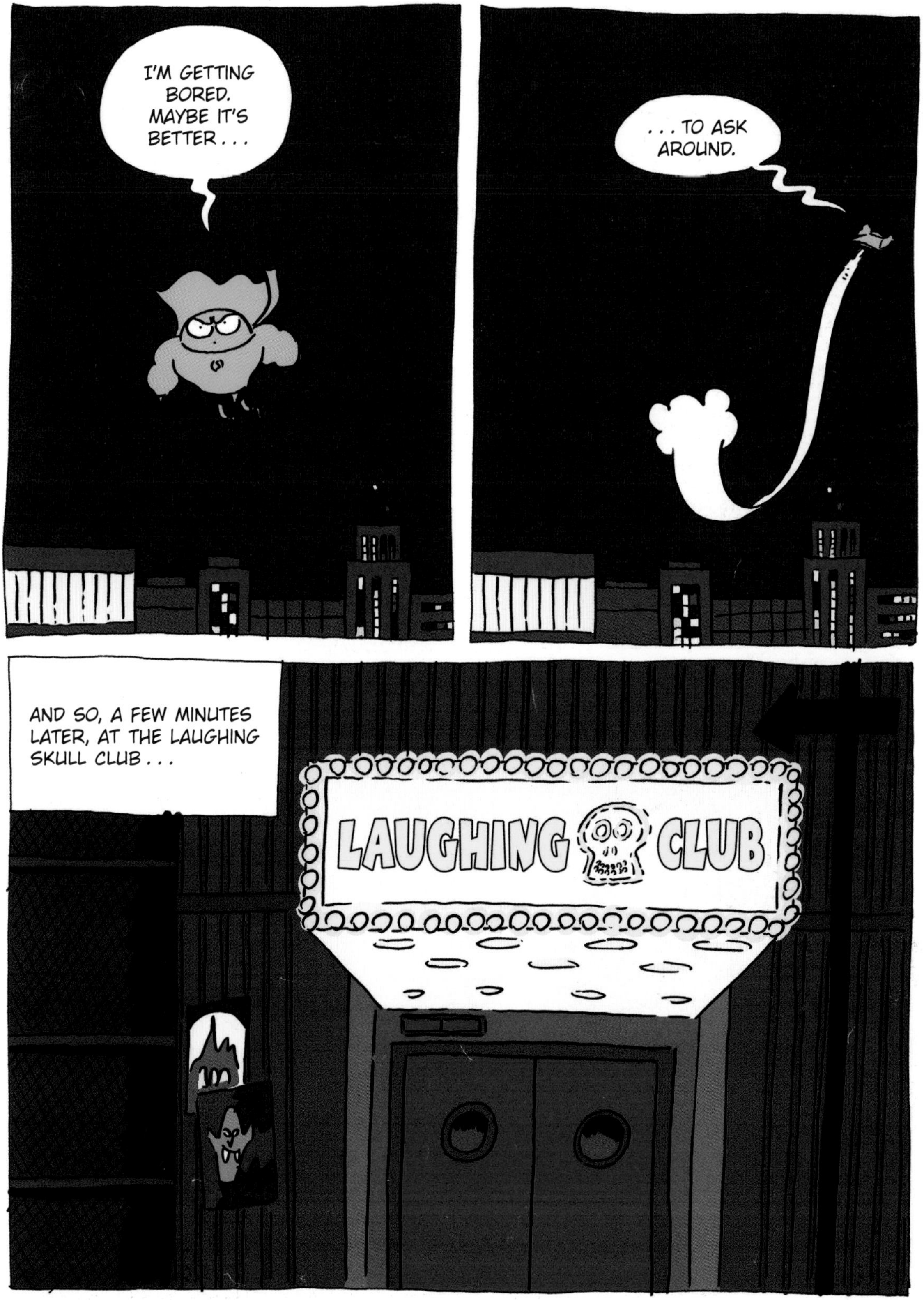
I'M GETTING BORED. MAYBE IT'S BETTER . . .
. . . TO ASK AROUND.
AND SO, A FEW MINUTES LATER, AT THE LAUGHING SKULL CLUB . . .
LAUGHING CLUB

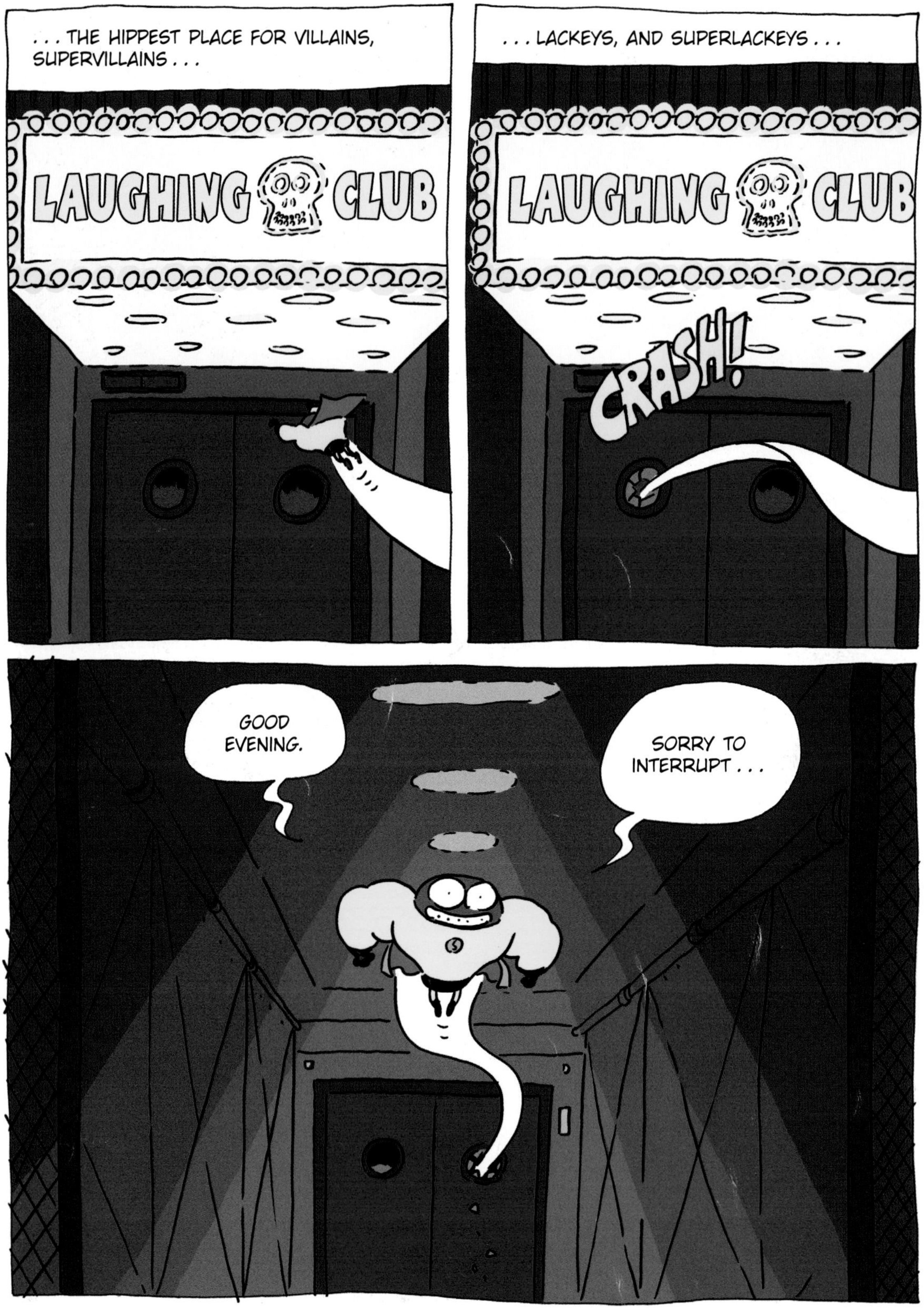
. . . THE HIPPEST PLACE FOR VILLAINS, SUPERVILLAINS . . .
LAUGHING CLUB
. . . LACKEYS, AND SUPERLACKEYS . . .
LAUGHING CLUB
CRASH!
GOOD EVENING.
SORRY TO INTERRUPT . . .

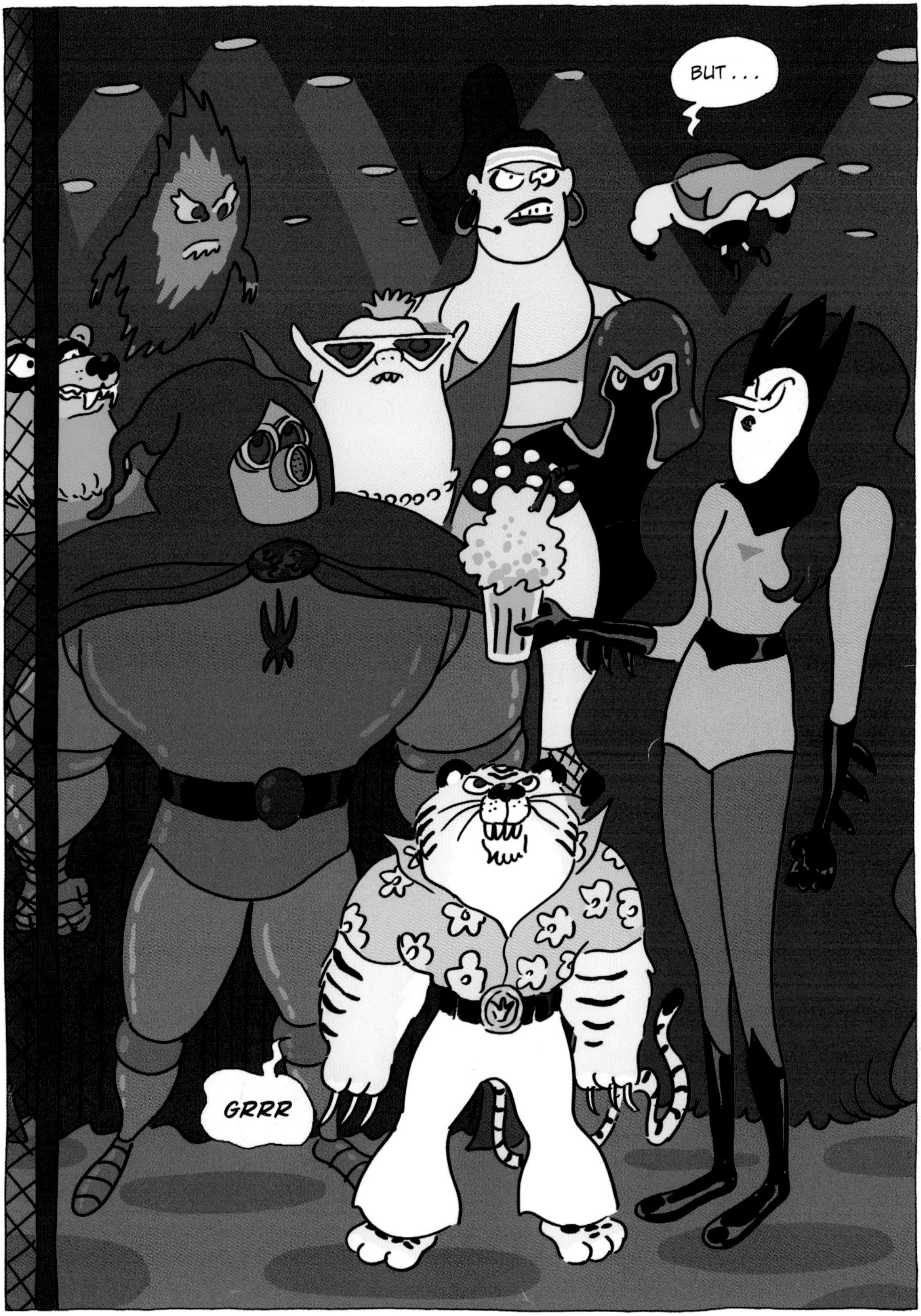
BUT . . .
GRRR

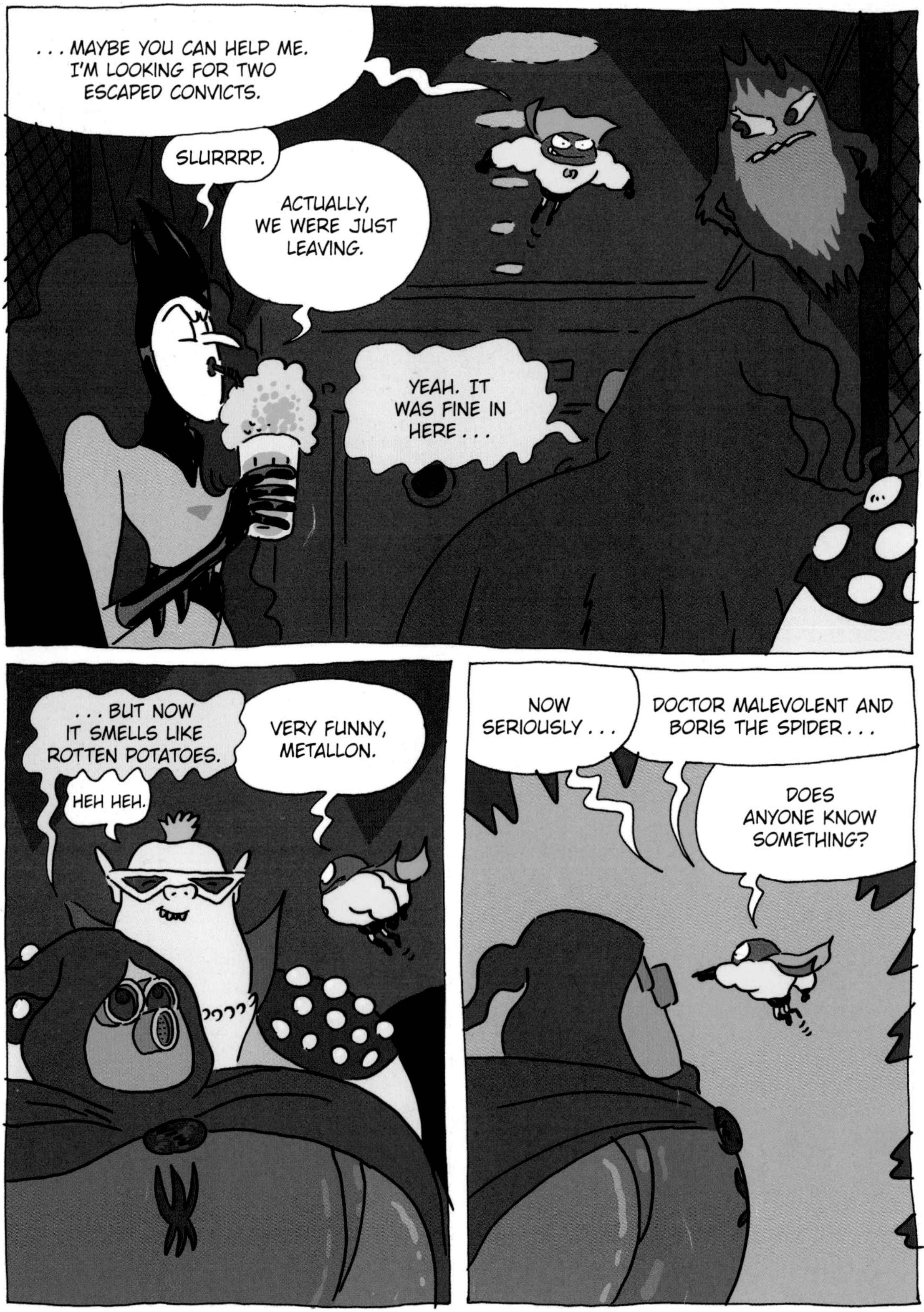
. . . MAYBE YOU CAN HELP ME. I'M LOOKING FOR TWO ESCAPED CONVICTS.
SLURRRP.
ACTUALLY, WE WERE JUST LEAVING.
YEAH. IT WAS FINE IN HERE . . .
. . . BUT NOW IT SMELLS LIKE ROTTEN POTATOES.
HEH HEH.
VERY FUNNY, METALLON.
NOW SERIOUSLY . . .
DOCTOR MALEVOLENT AND BORIS THE SPIDER . . .
DOES ANYONE KNOW SOMETHING?

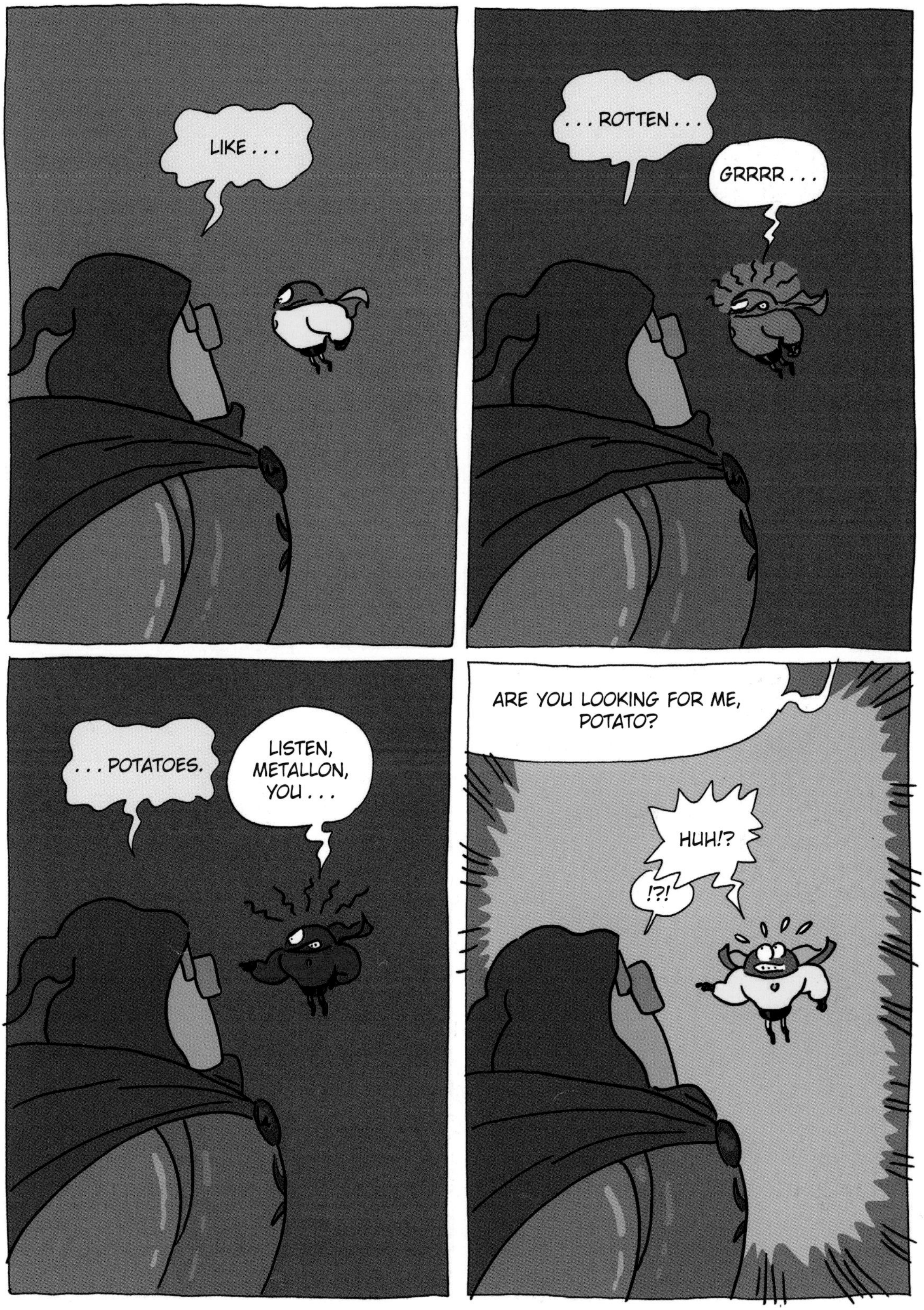
LIKE . . .
. . . ROTTEN . . .
GRRRR . . .
. . . POTATOES.
LISTEN, METALLON, YOU . . .
ARE YOU LOOKING FOR ME, POTATO?
HUH!?
!?!

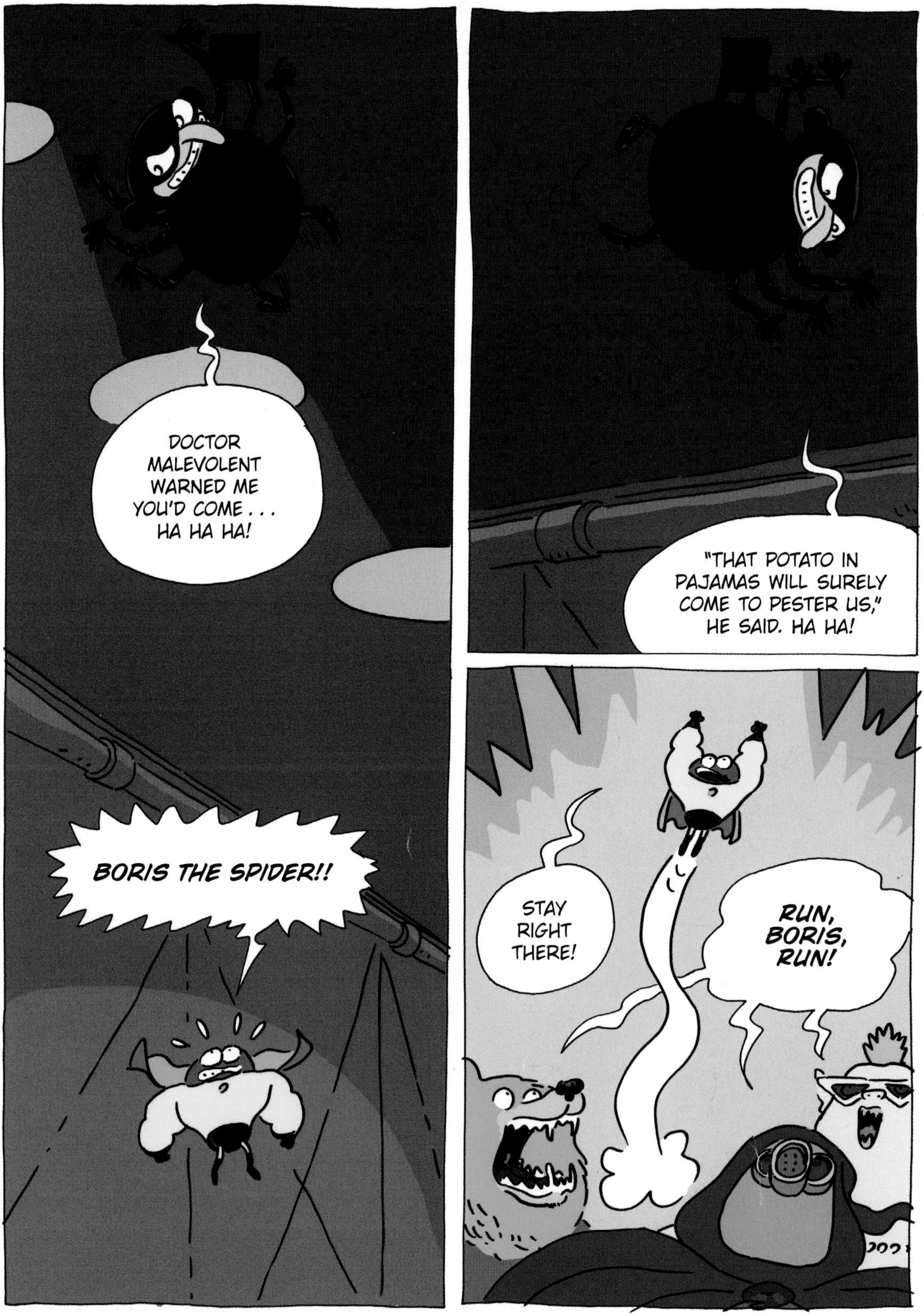
DOCTOR MALEVOLENT WARNED ME YOU'D COME . . . HA HA HA!
"THAT POTATO IN PAJAMAS WILL SURELY COME TO PESTER US," HE SAID. HA HA!
BORIS THE SPIDER!!
STAY RIGHT THERE!
RUN, BORIS, RUN!

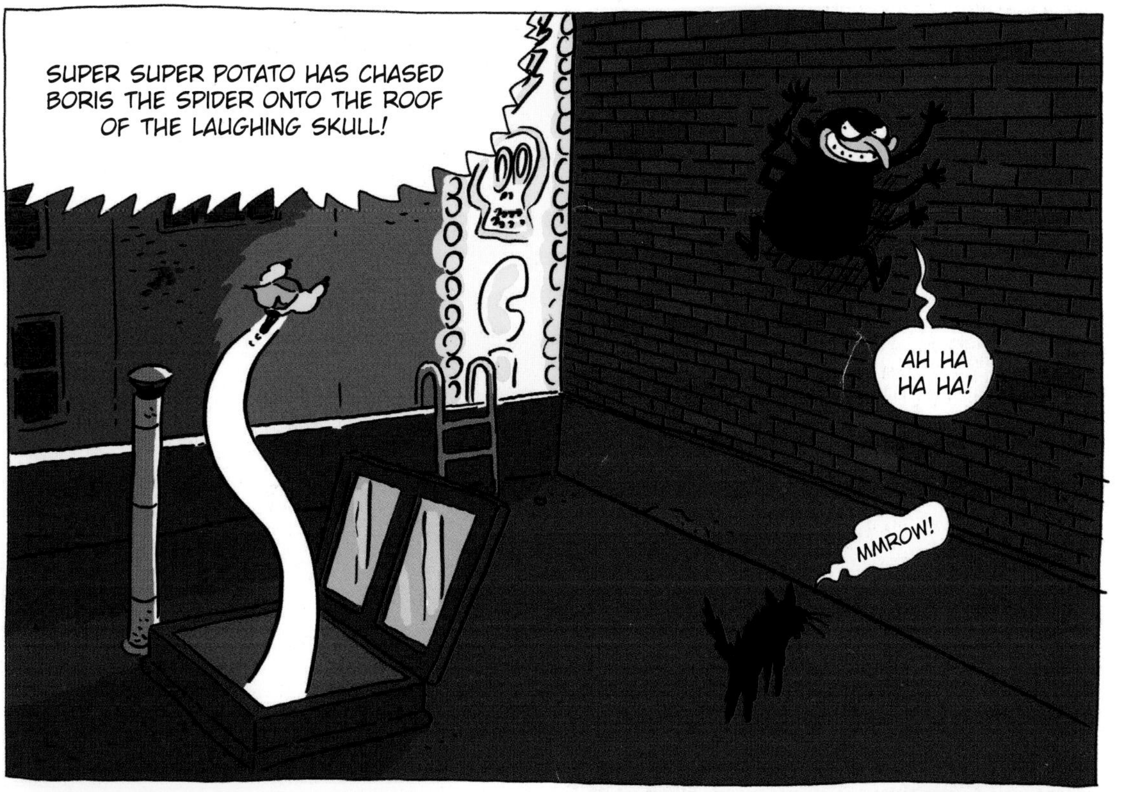
SUPER SUPER POTATO HAS CHASED BORIS THE SPIDER ONTO THE ROOF OF THE LAUGHING SKULL!
AH HA HA HA!
MMROW!

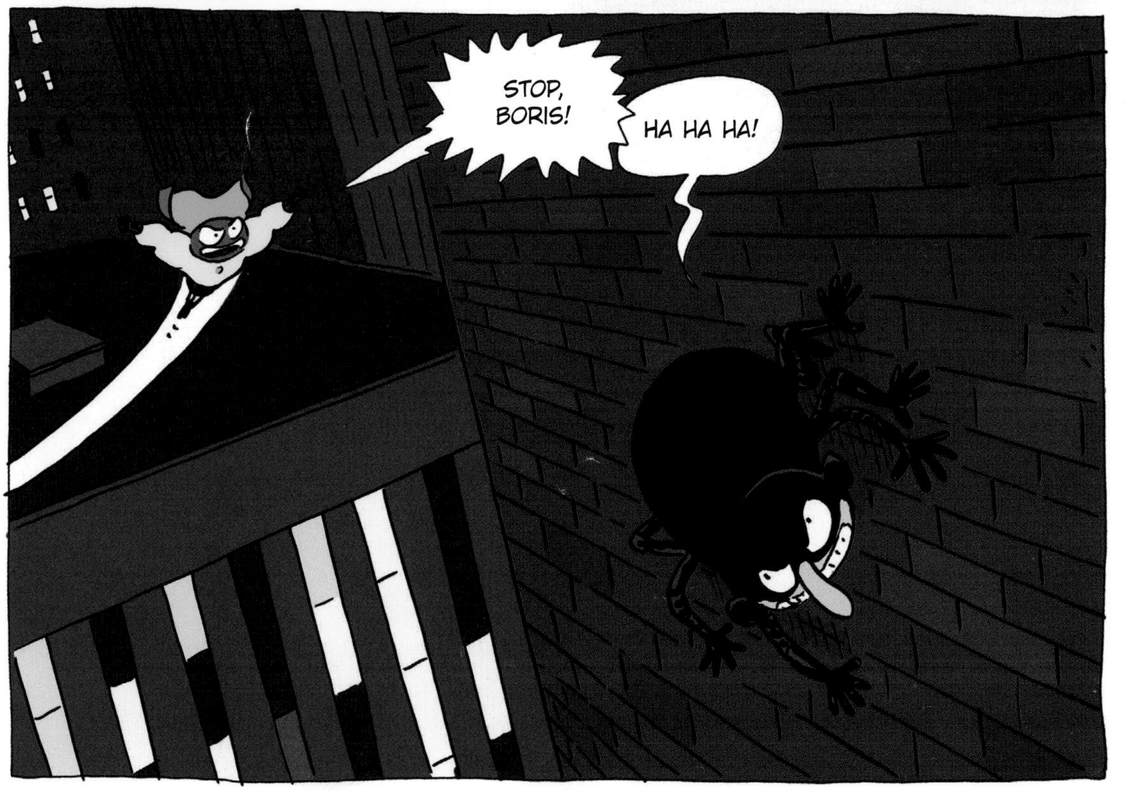
STOP, BORIS!
HA HA HA!

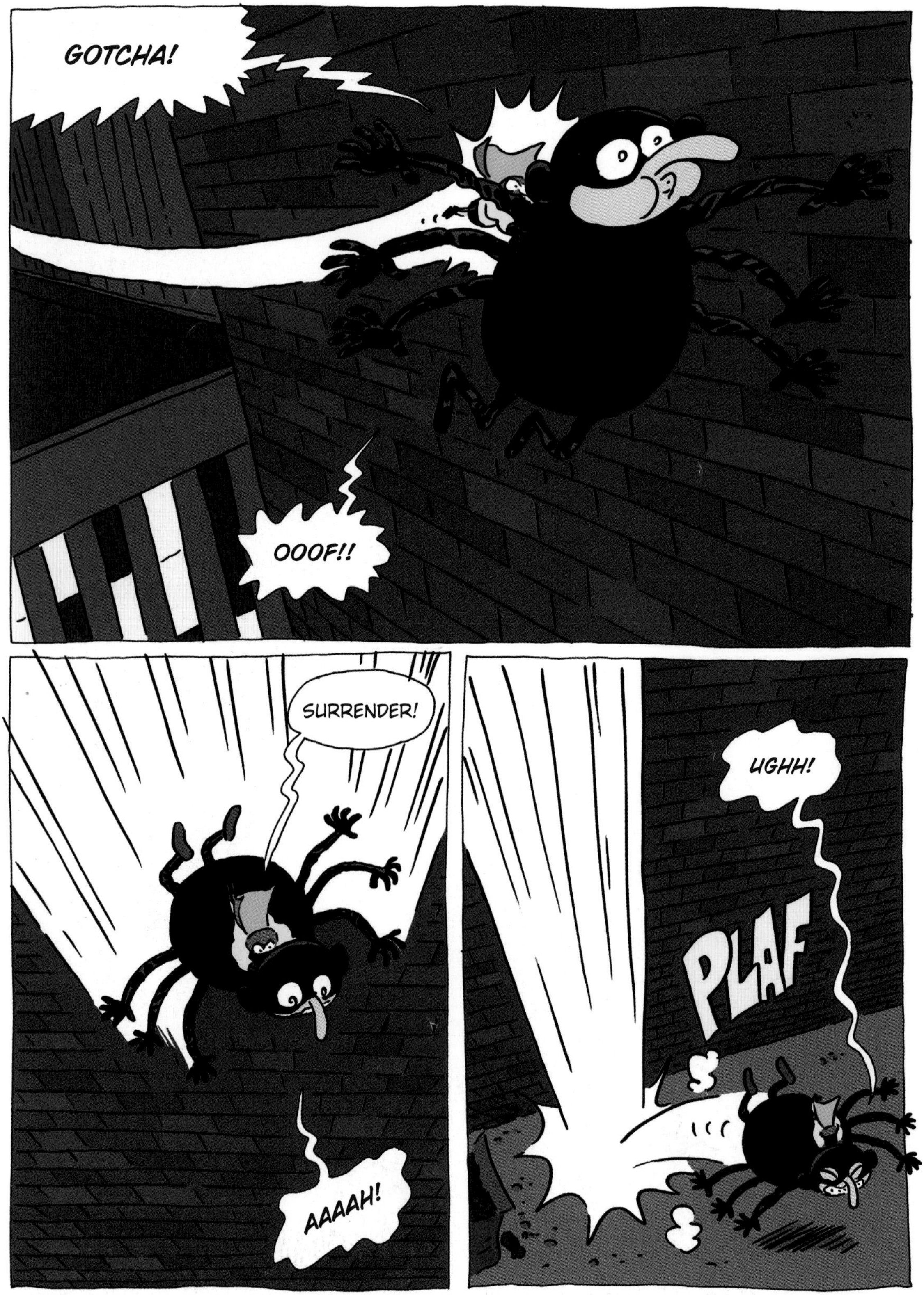
GOTCHA!
OOOF!!
SURRENDER!
AAAAH!
UGHH!
PLAF

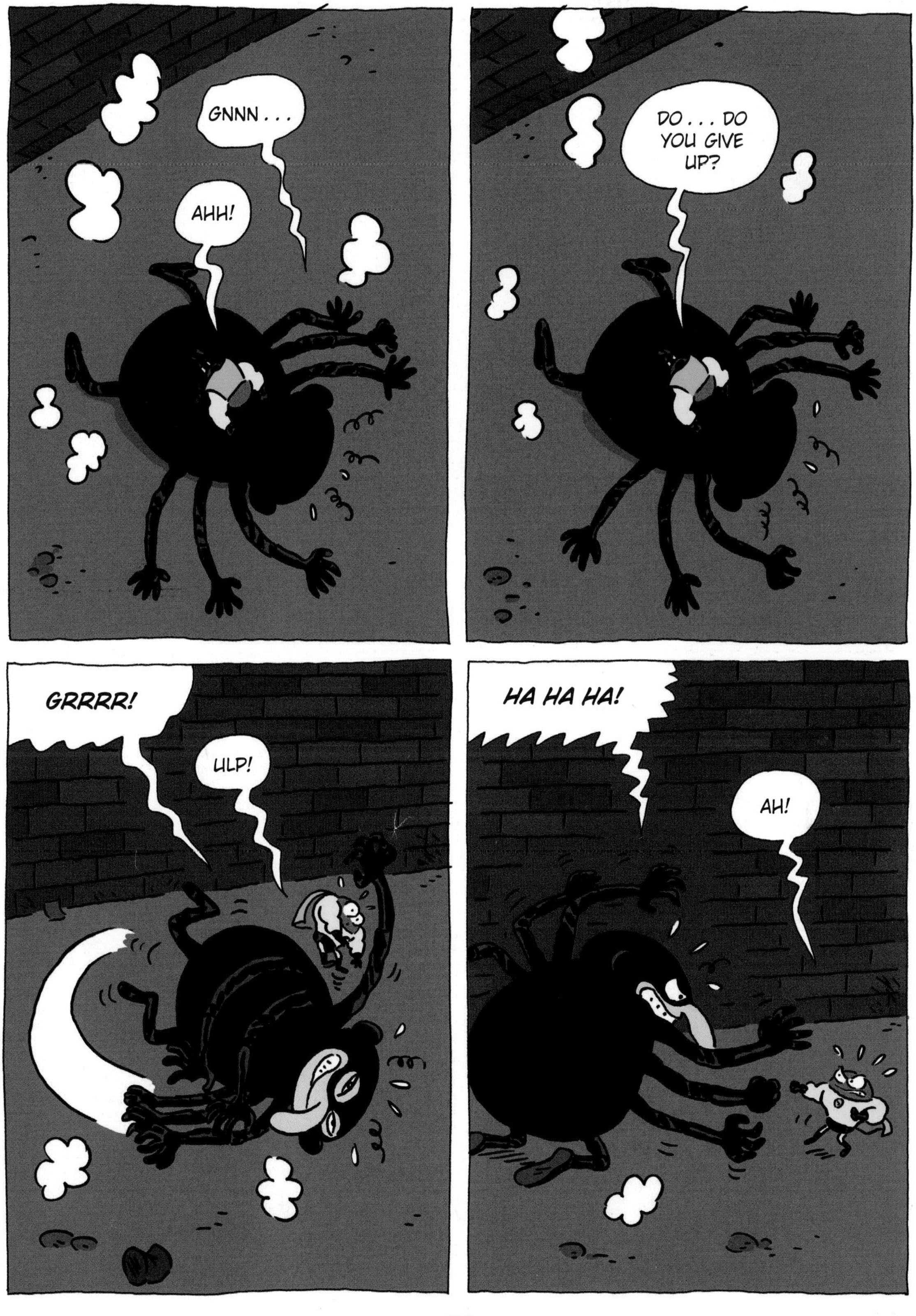
GNNN . . .
AHH!
DO . . . DO YOU GIVE UP?
GRRRR!
ULP!
HA HA HA!
AH!

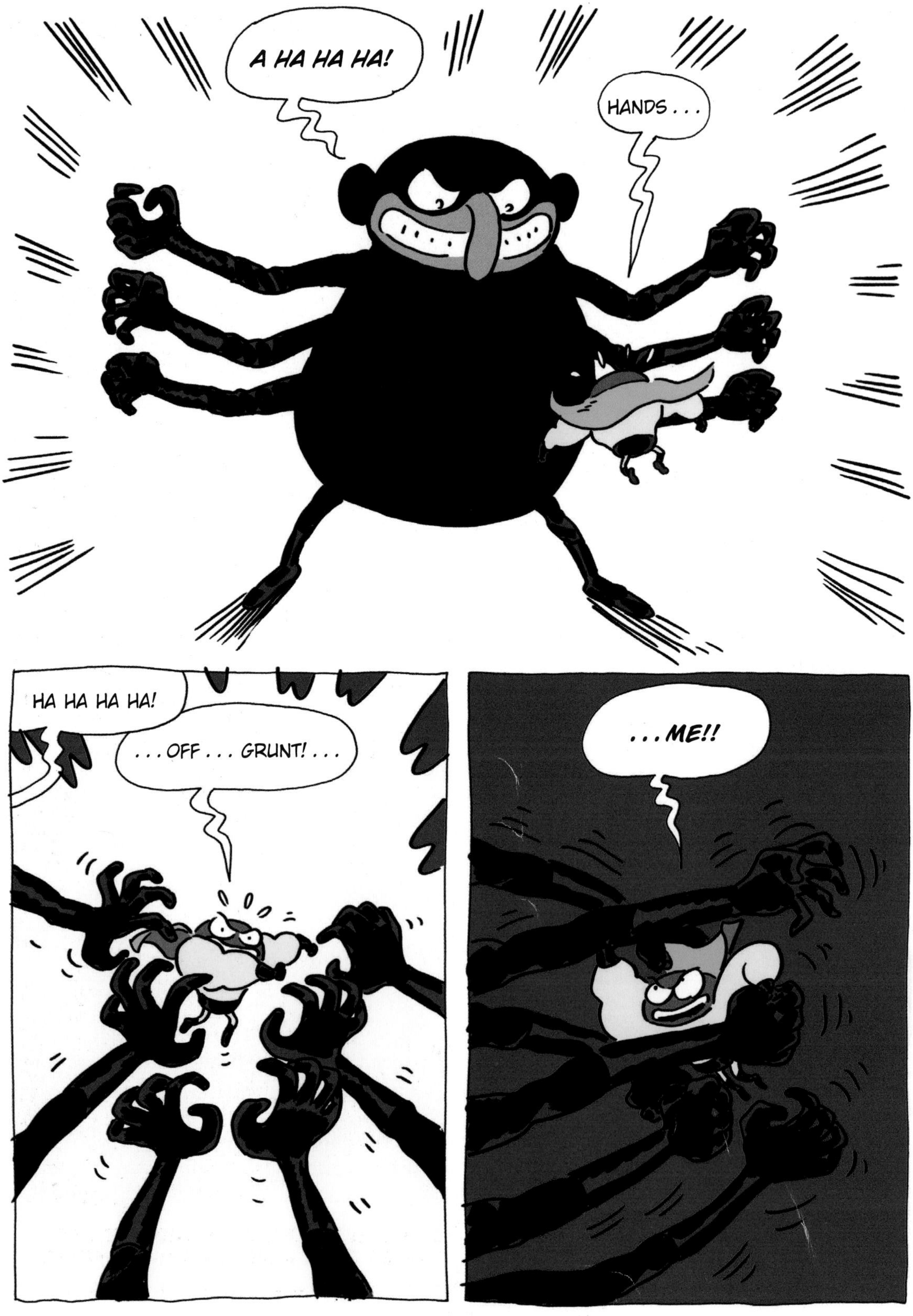
A HA HA HA!
HANDS . . .
HA HA HA HA!
. . . OFF . . . GRUNT! . . .
. . . ME!!

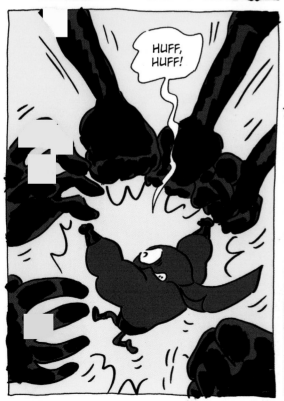

SUPER SUPER POTATO IS STARTING TO GET TANGLED IN THE ARMS OF BORIS THE SPIDER.

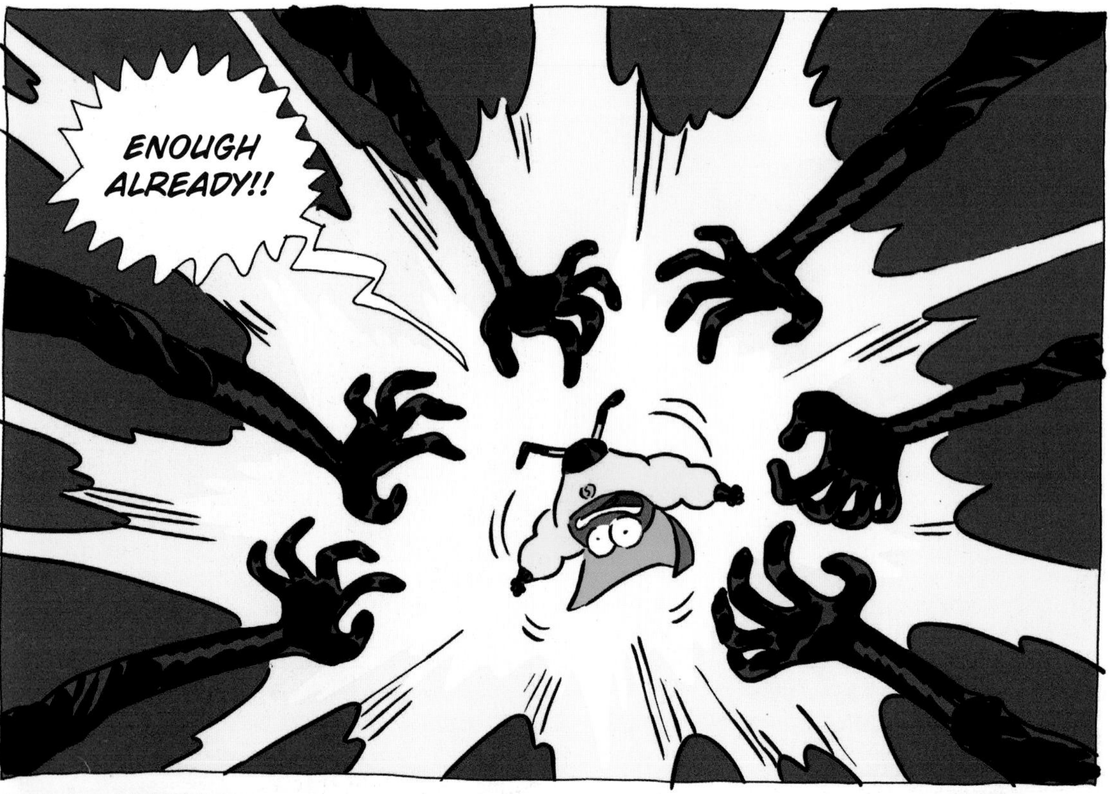
ENOUGH ALREADY!!

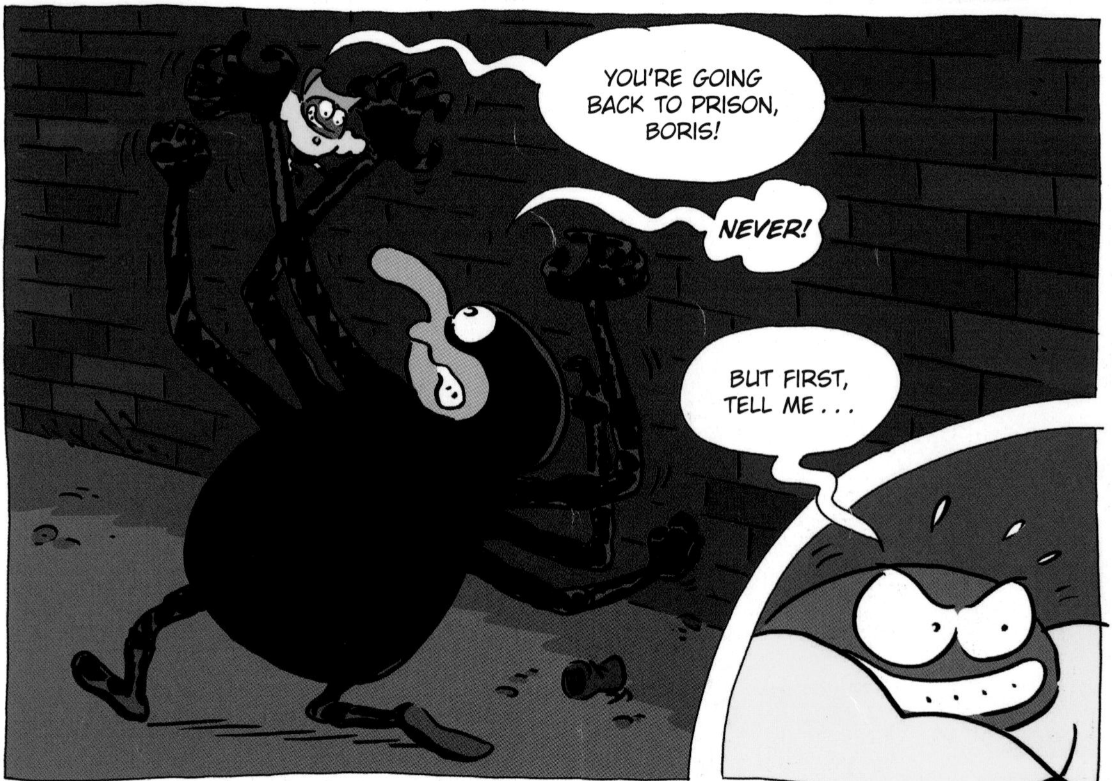
YOU'RE GOING BACK TO PRISON, BORIS!
NEVER!
BUT FIRST, TELL ME . . .

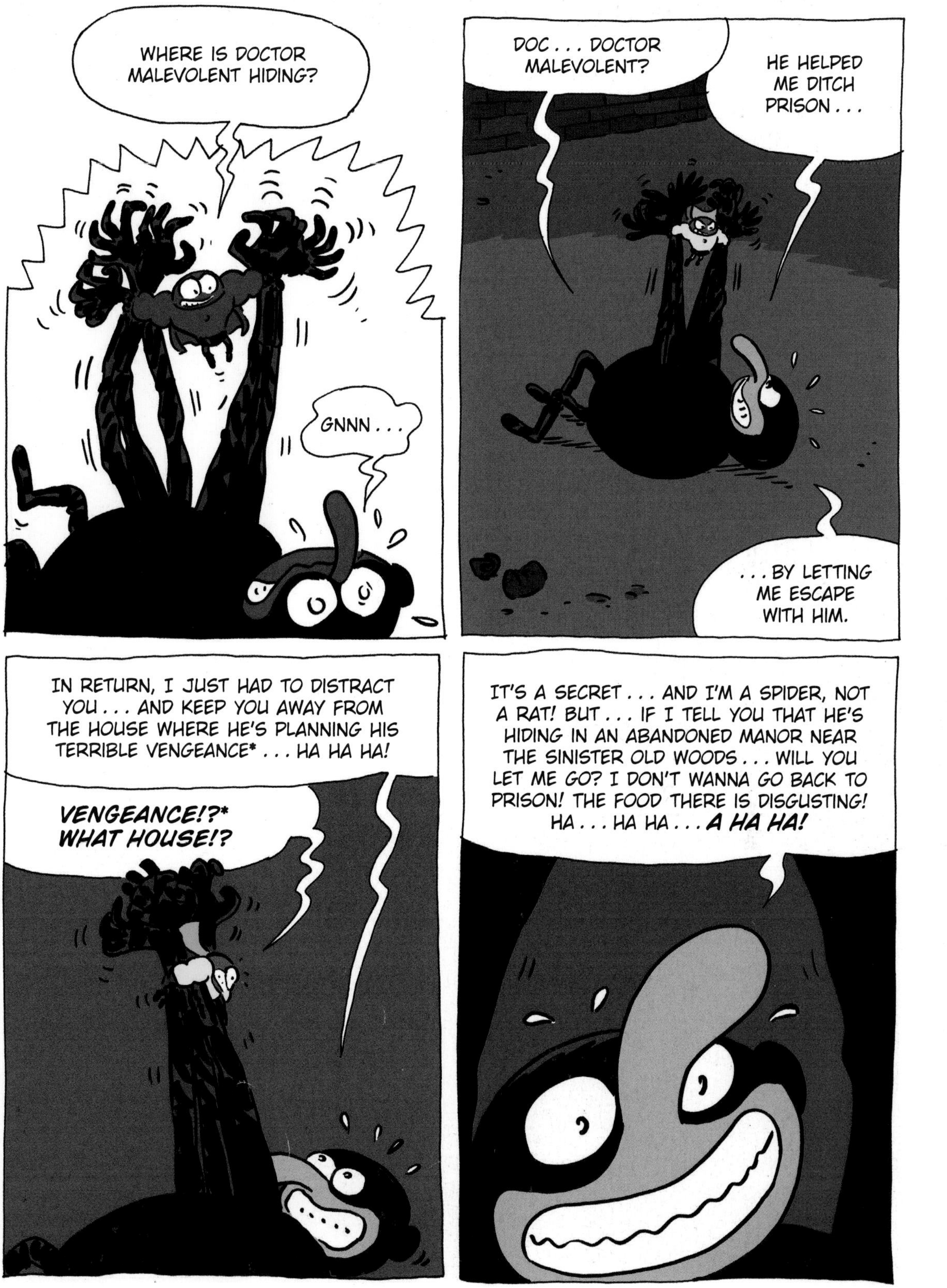

WHERE IS DOCTOR MALEVOLENT HIDING?
GNNN . . .
DOC . . . DOCTOR MALEVOLENT?
HE HELPED ME DITCH PRISON . . .
. . . BY LETTING ME ESCAPE WITH HIM.
IN RETURN, I JUST HAD TO DISTRACT YOU . . . AND KEEP YOU AWAY FROM THE HOUSE WHERE HE'S PLANNING HIS TERRIBLE VENGEANCE* . . . HA HA HA!
VENGEANCE!?* WHAT HOUSE!?
IT'S A SECRET . . . AND I'M A SPIDER, NOT A RAT! BUT . . . IF I TELL YOU THAT HE'S HIDING IN AN ABANDONED MANOR NEAR THE SINISTER OLD WOODS . . . WILL YOU LET ME GO? I DON'T WANNA GO BACK TO PRISON! THE FOOD THERE IS DISGUSTING! HA . . . HA HA . . . A HA HA!

* "TERRIBLE VENGEANCE" WERE THE DOCTOR'S EXACT WORDS.

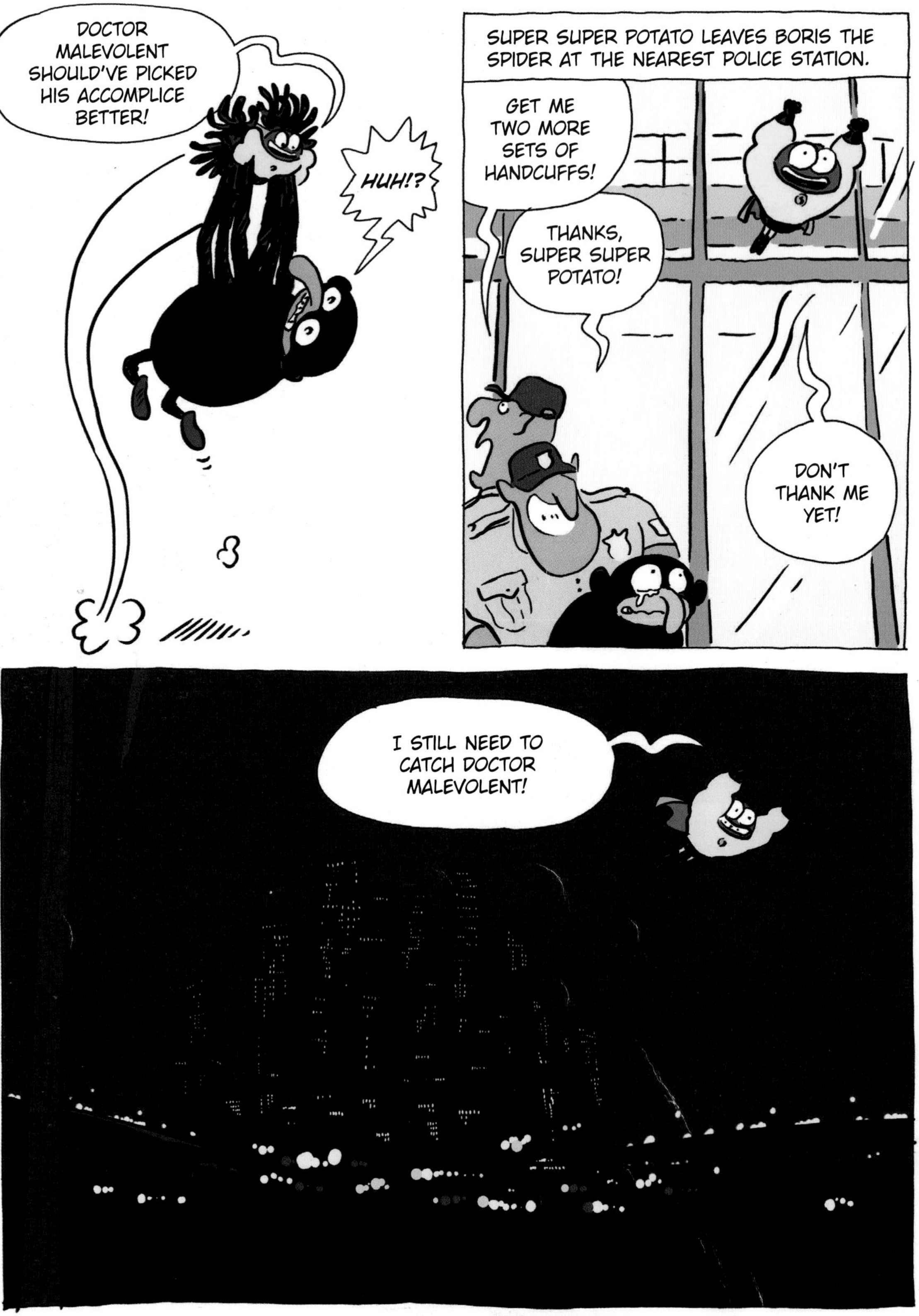
DOCTOR MALEVOLENT SHOULD'VE PICKED HIS ACCOMPLICE BETTER!
HUH!?
SUPER SUPER POTATO LEAVES BORIS THE SPIDER AT THE NEAREST POLICE STATION.
GET ME TWO MORE SETS OF HANDCUFFS!
THANKS, SUPER SUPER POTATO!
DON'T THANK ME YET!
I STILL NEED TO CATCH DOCTOR MALEVOLENT!

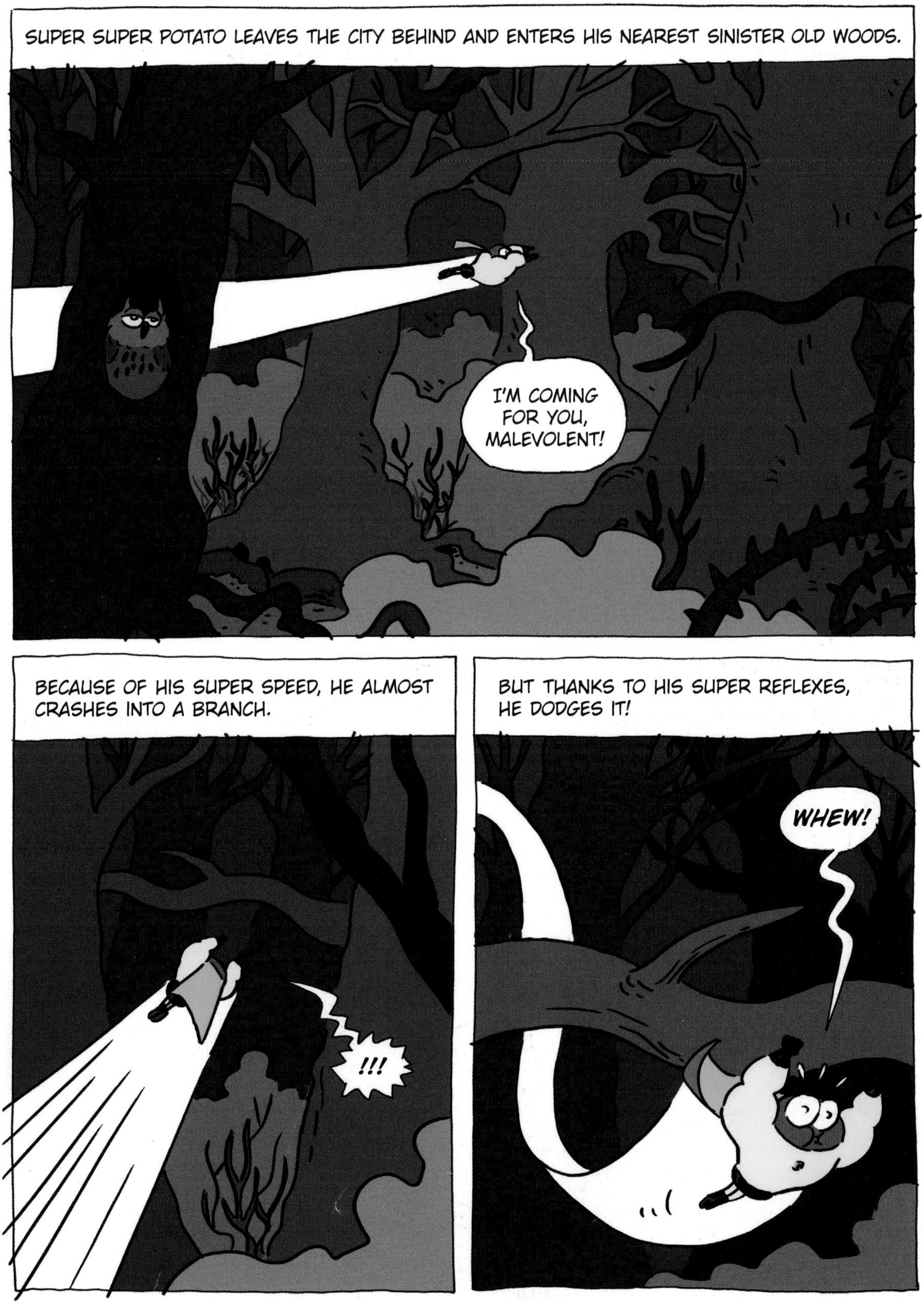
SUPER SUPER POTATO LEAVES THE CITY BEHIND AND ENTERS HIS NEAREST SINISTER OLD WOODS.
I'M COMING FOR YOU, MALEVOLENT!
BECAUSE OF HIS SUPER SPEED, HE ALMOST CRASHES INTO A BRANCH.
!!!
BUT THANKS TO HIS SUPER REFLEXES, HE DODGES IT!
WHEW!

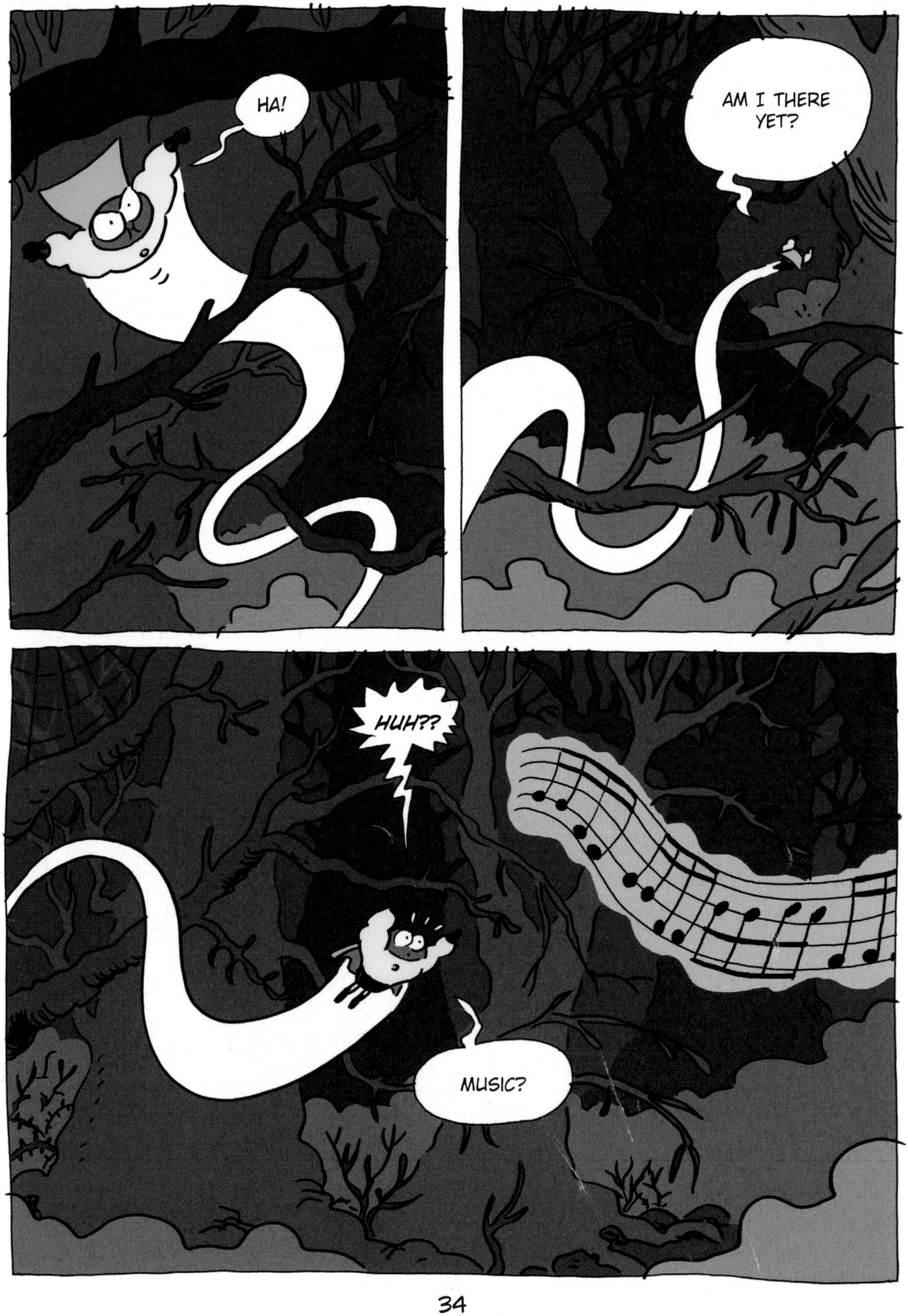
HA!
AM I THERE YET?
HUH??
MUSIC?

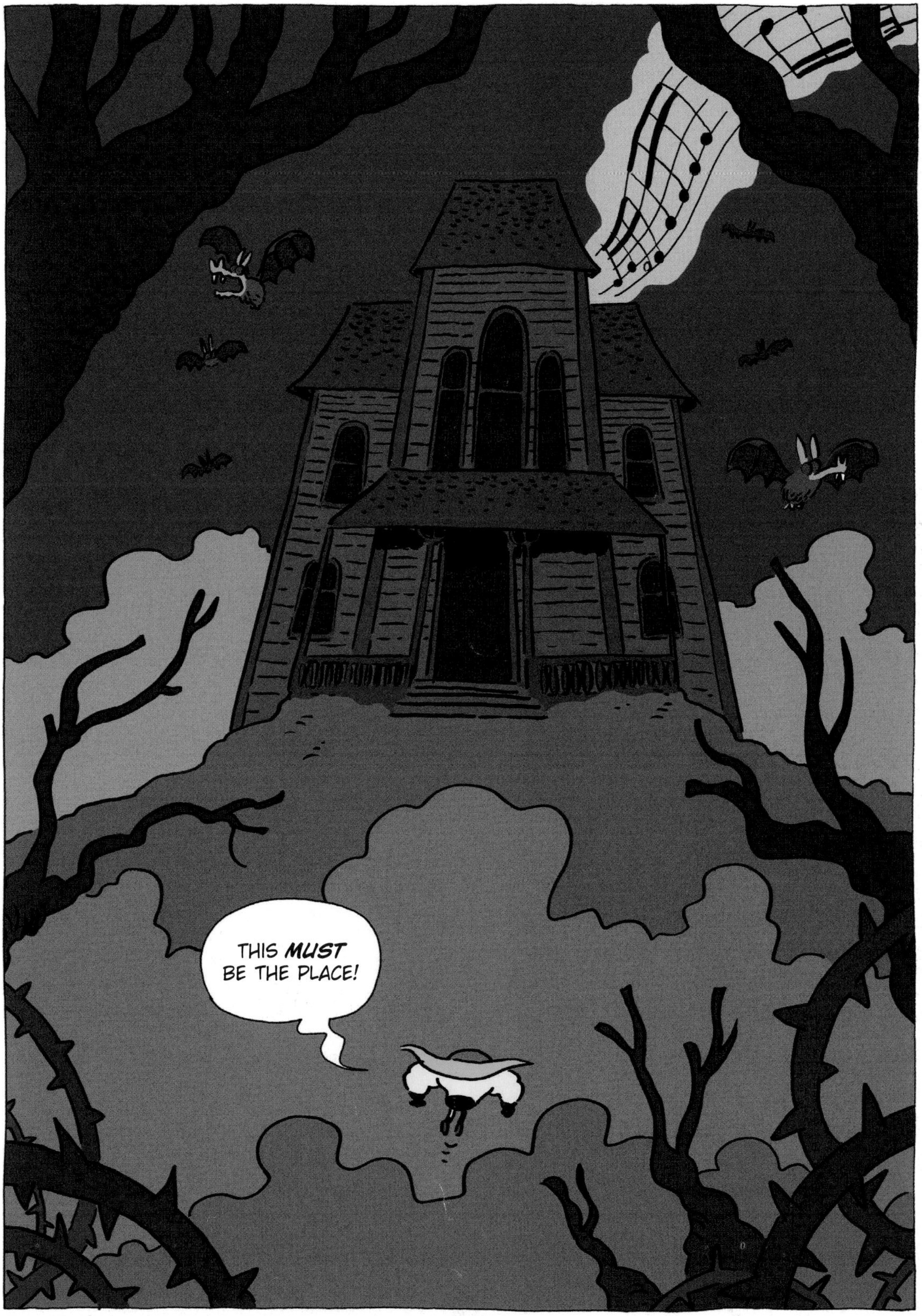
THIS **MUST** BE THE PLACE!

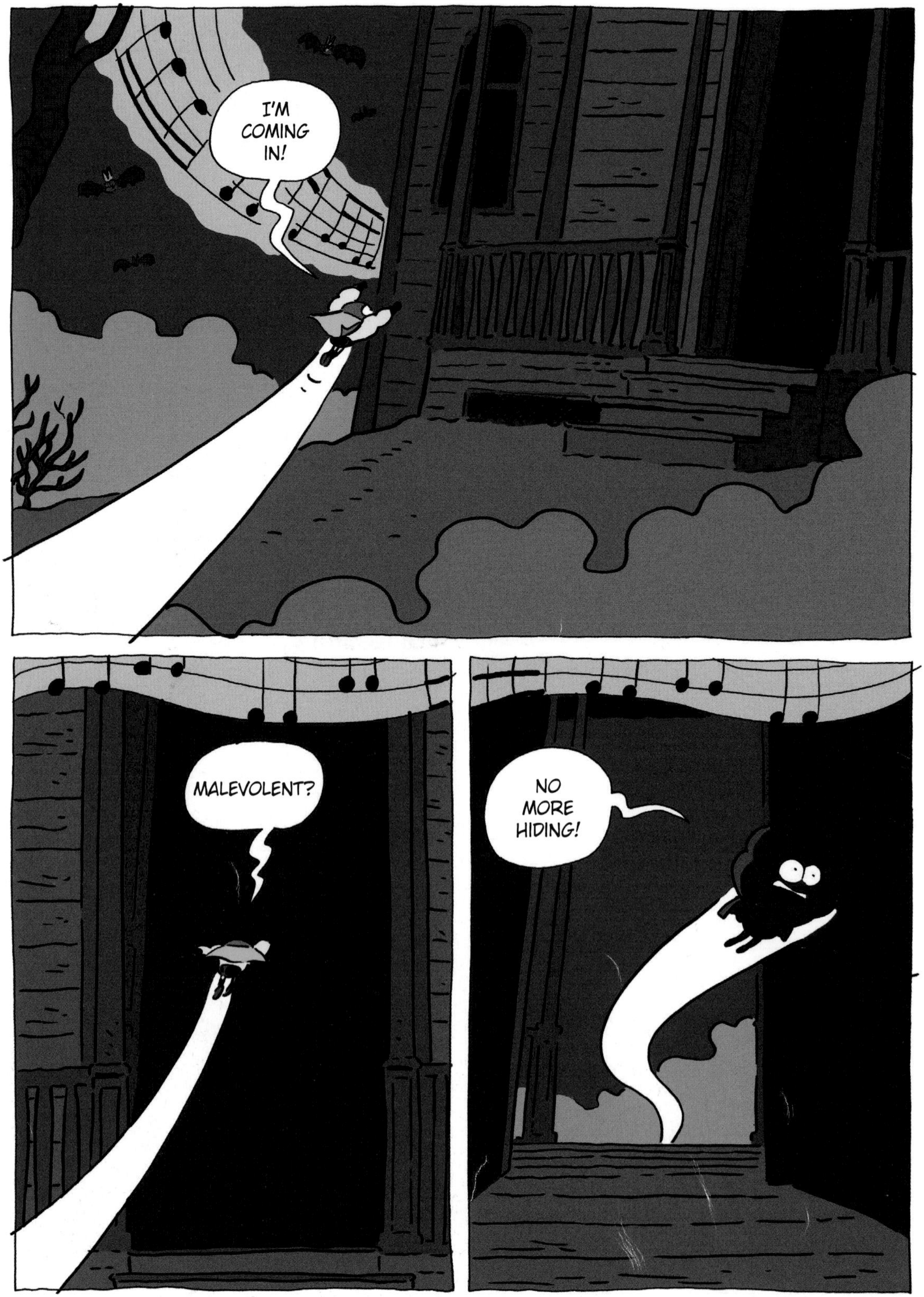
I'M COMING IN!
MALEVOLENT?
NO MORE HIDING!

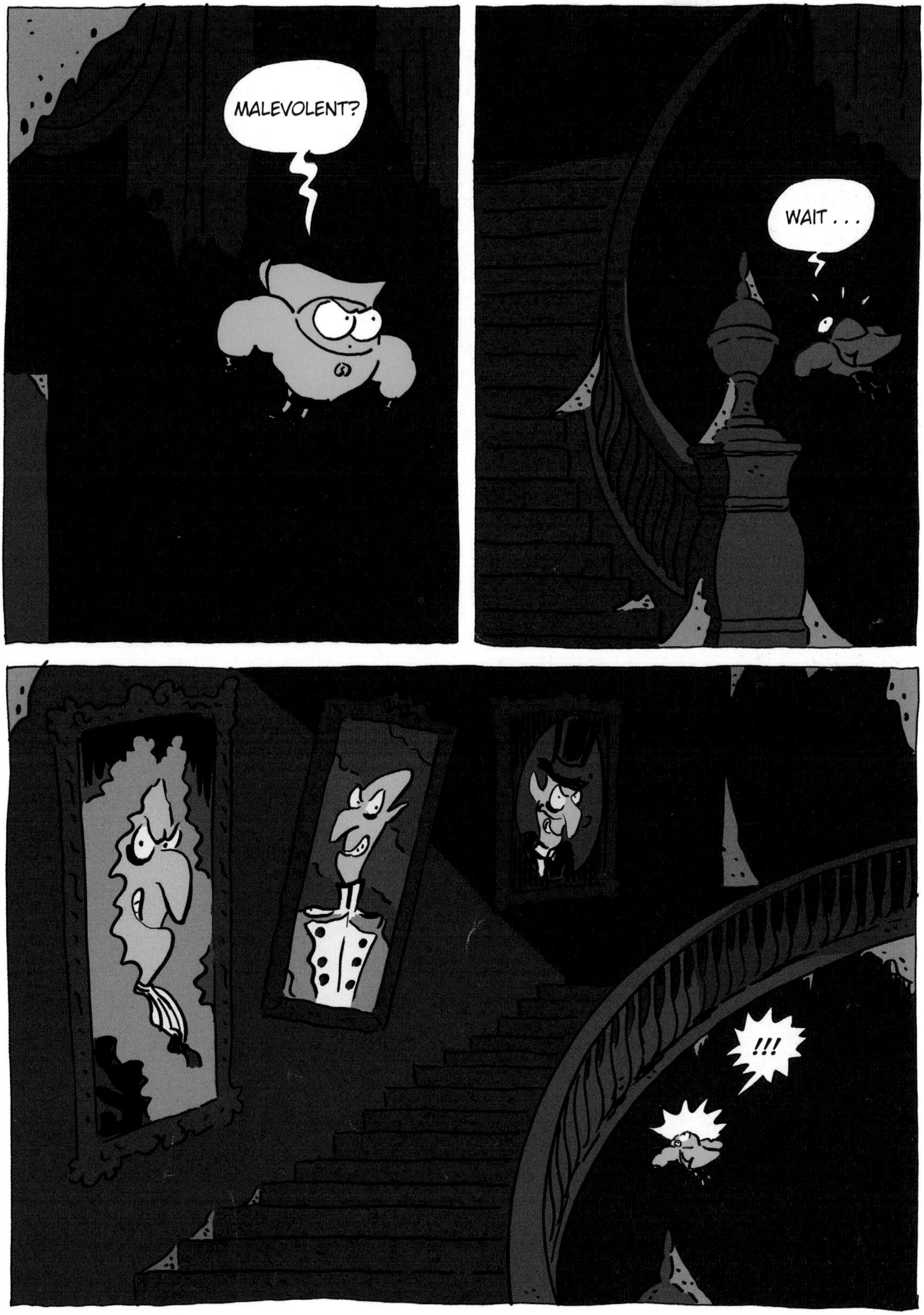
MALEVOLENT?
WAIT . . .
!!!

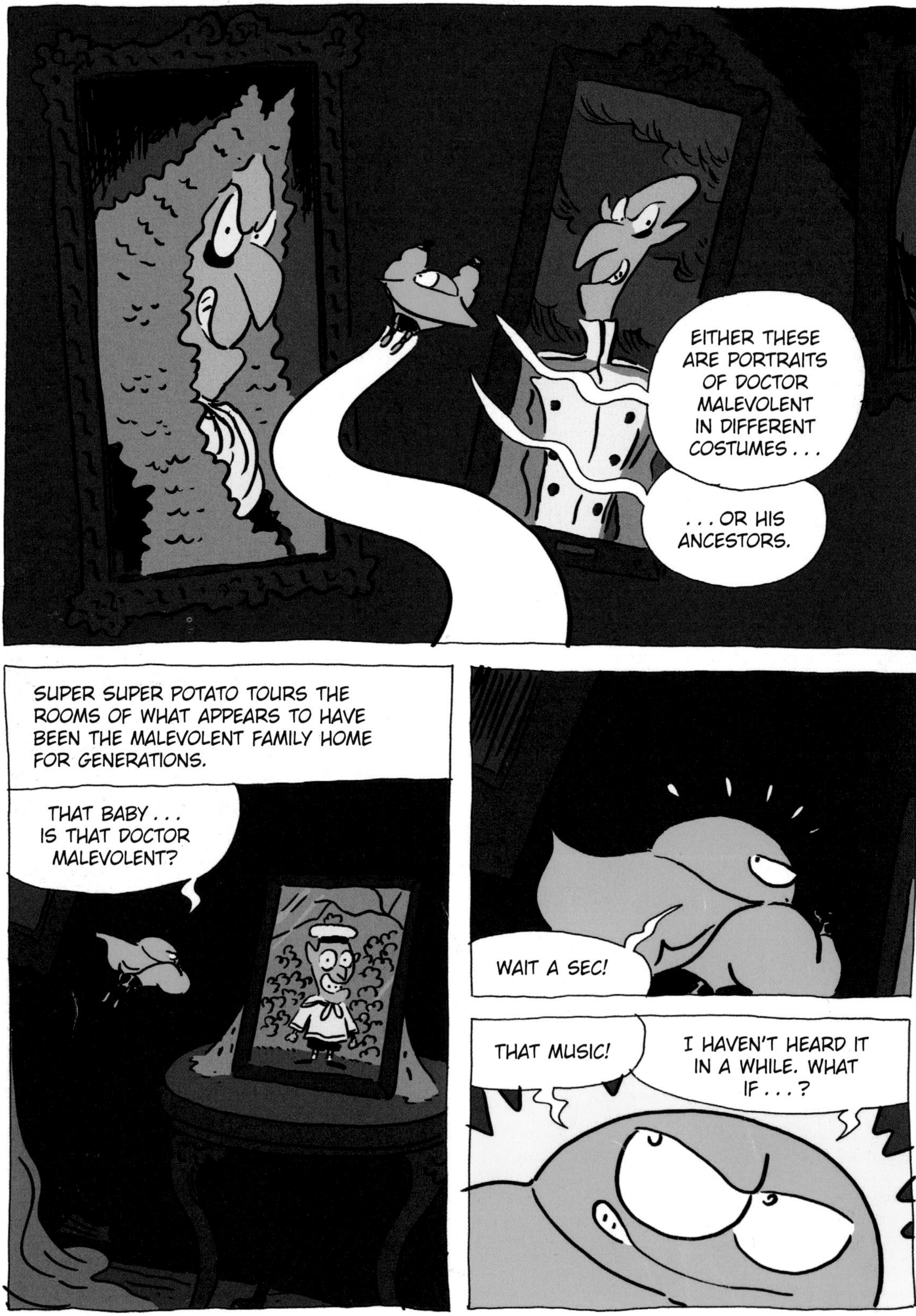
EITHER THESE ARE PORTRAITS OF DOCTOR MALEVOLENT IN DIFFERENT COSTUMES . . .
. . . OR HIS ANCESTORS.
SUPER SUPER POTATO TOURS THE ROOMS OF WHAT APPEARS TO HAVE BEEN THE MALEVOLENT FAMILY HOME FOR GENERATIONS.
THAT BABY . . . IS THAT DOCTOR MALEVOLENT?
WAIT A SEC!
THAT MUSIC!
I HAVEN'T HEARD IT IN A WHILE. WHAT IF . . . ?

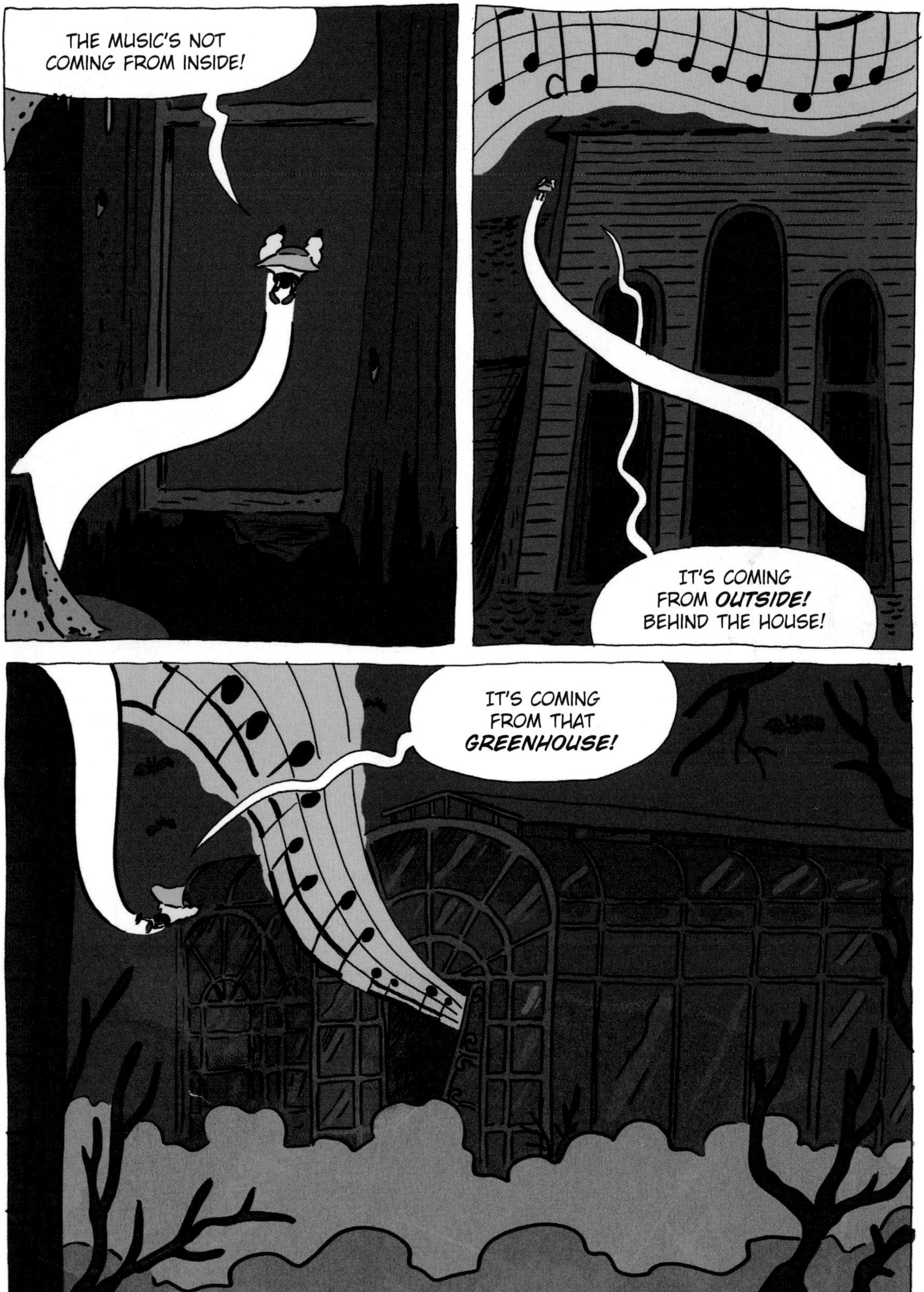
THE MUSIC'S NOT COMING FROM INSIDE!
IT'S COMING FROM **OUTSIDE!** BEHIND THE HOUSE!
IT'S COMING FROM THAT **GREENHOUSE!**

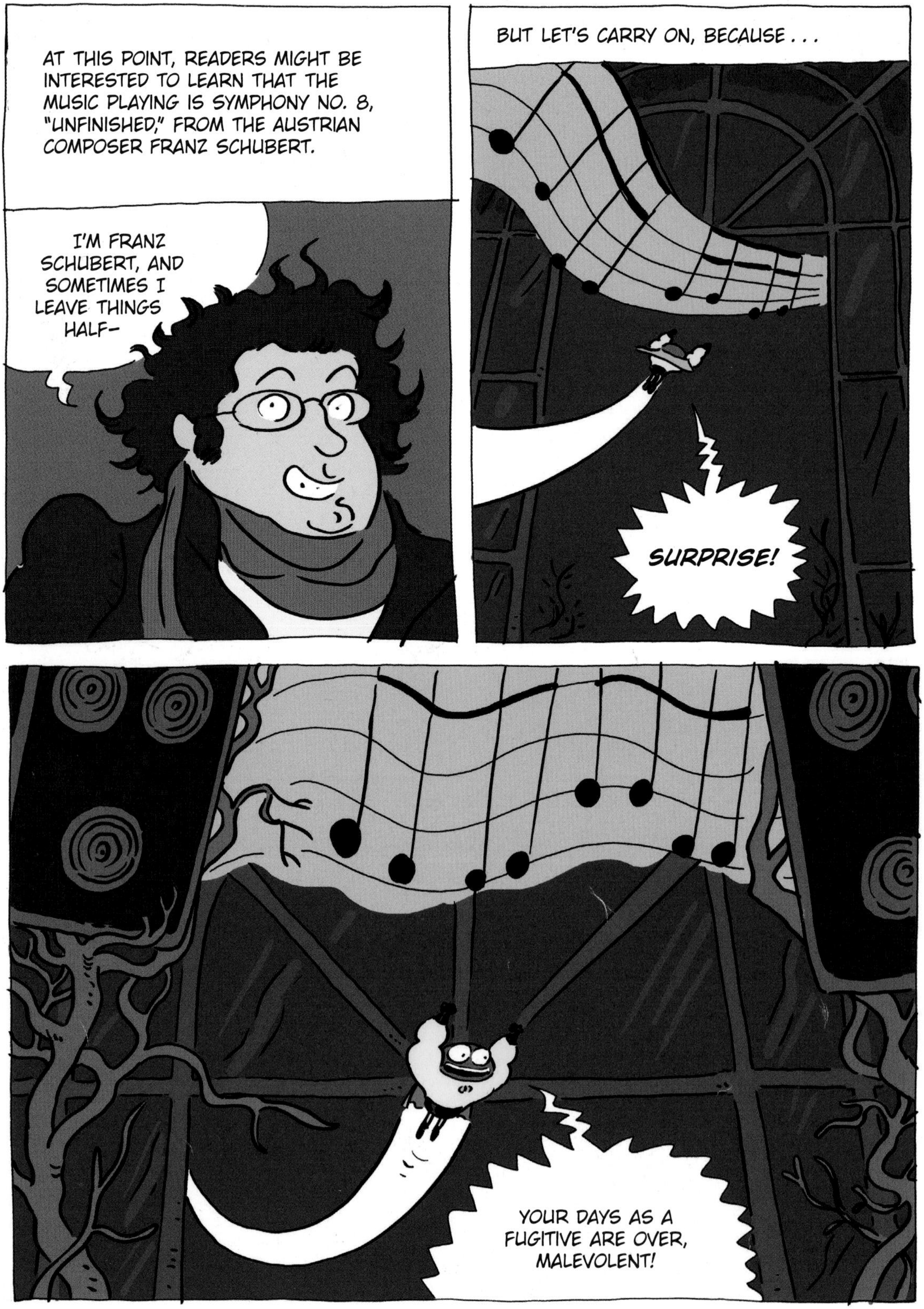
AT THIS POINT, READERS MIGHT BE INTERESTED TO LEARN THAT THE MUSIC PLAYING IS SYMPHONY NO. 8, "UNFINISHED," FROM THE AUSTRIAN COMPOSER FRANZ SCHUBERT.
I'M FRANZ SCHUBERT, AND SOMETIMES I LEAVE THINGS HALF-
BUT LET'S CARRY ON, BECAUSE . . .
SURPRISE!
YOUR DAYS AS A FUGITIVE ARE OVER, MALEVOLENT!

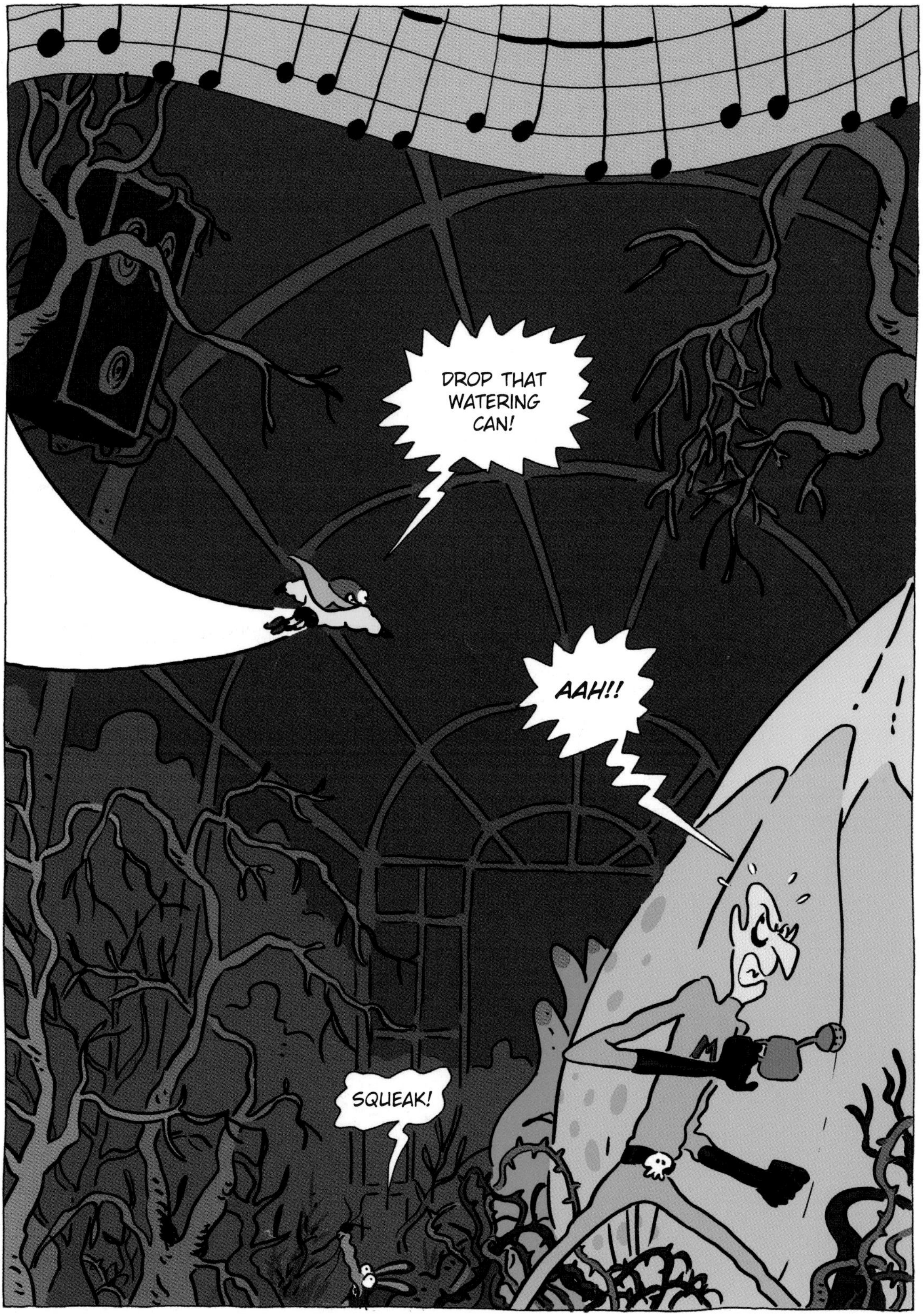
DROP THAT WATERING CAN!
AAH!!
SQUEAK!

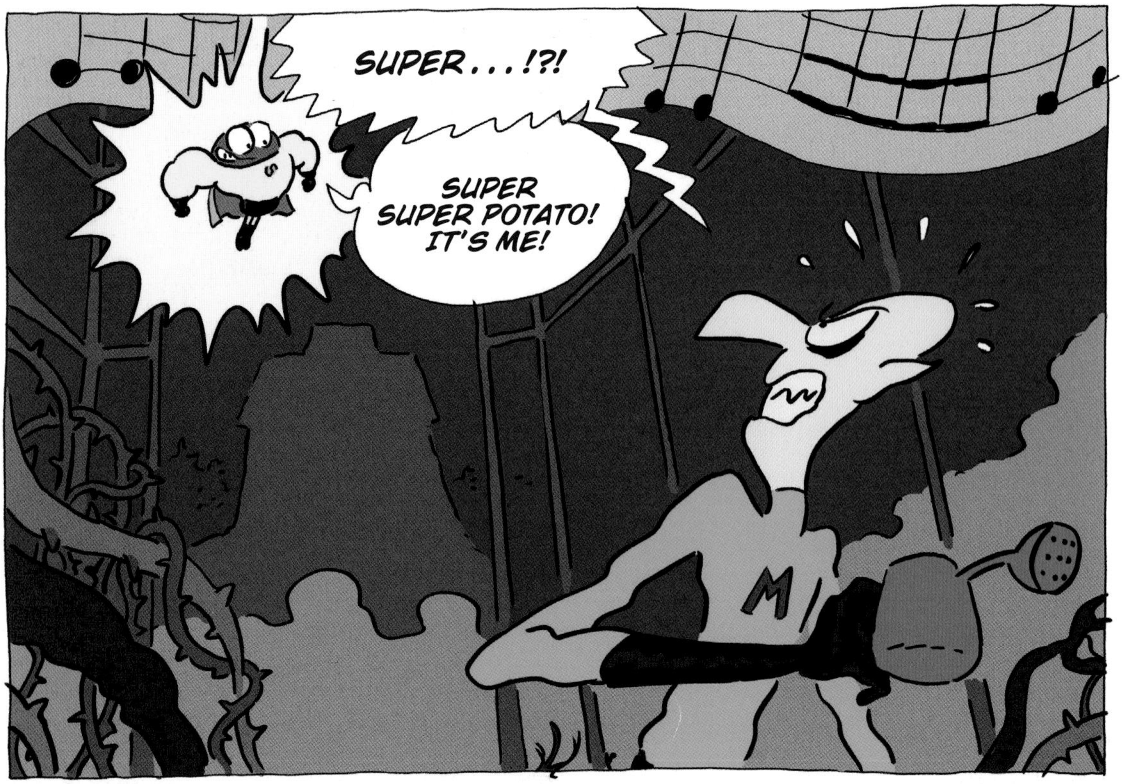
SUPER . . . !?!
SUPER SUPER POTATO! IT'S ME!

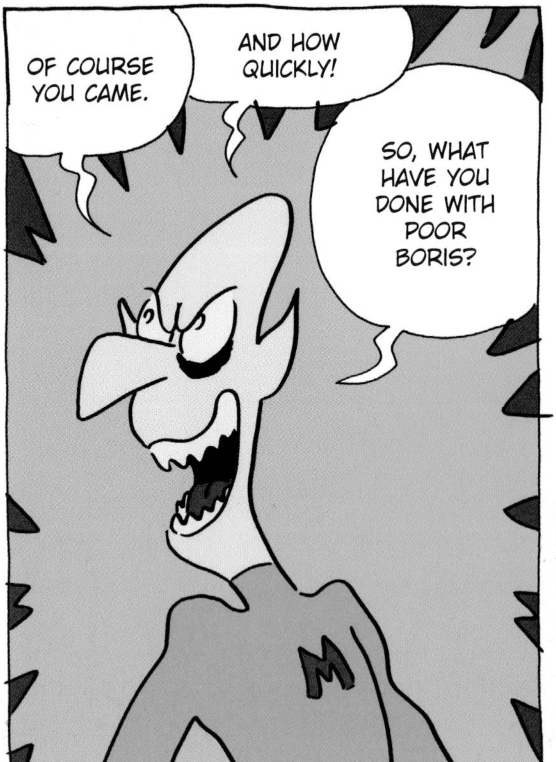
OF COURSE YOU CAME.
AND HOW QUICKLY!
SO, WHAT HAVE YOU DONE WITH POOR BORIS?

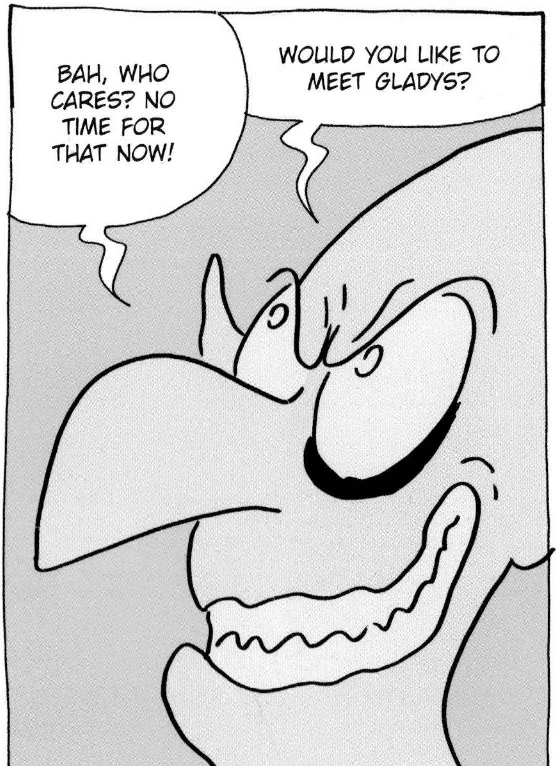
BAH, WHO CARES? NO TIME FOR THAT NOW!
WOULD YOU LIKE TO MEET GLADYS?

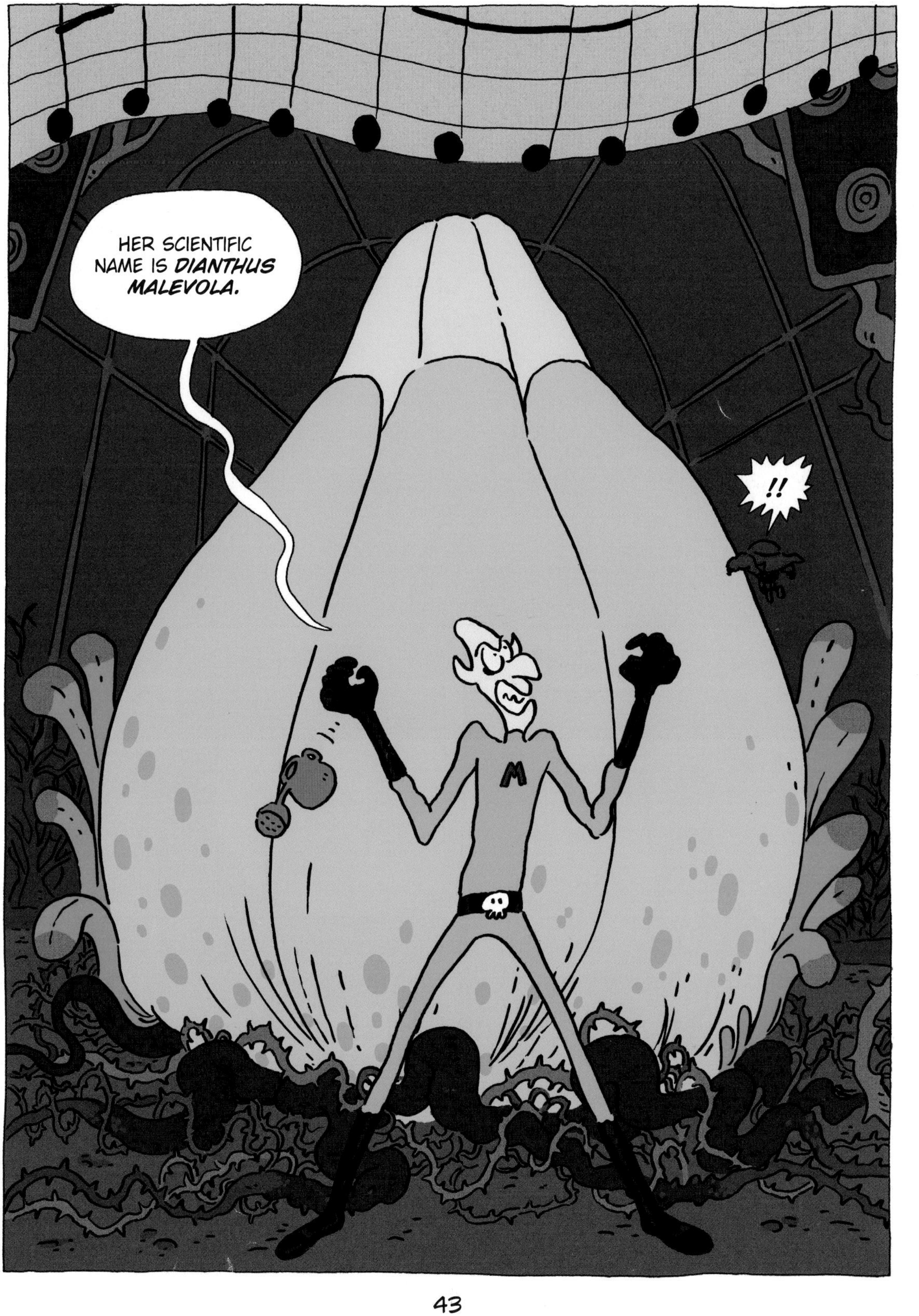
HER SCIENTIFIC NAME IS *DIANTHUS MALEVOLA.*
!!

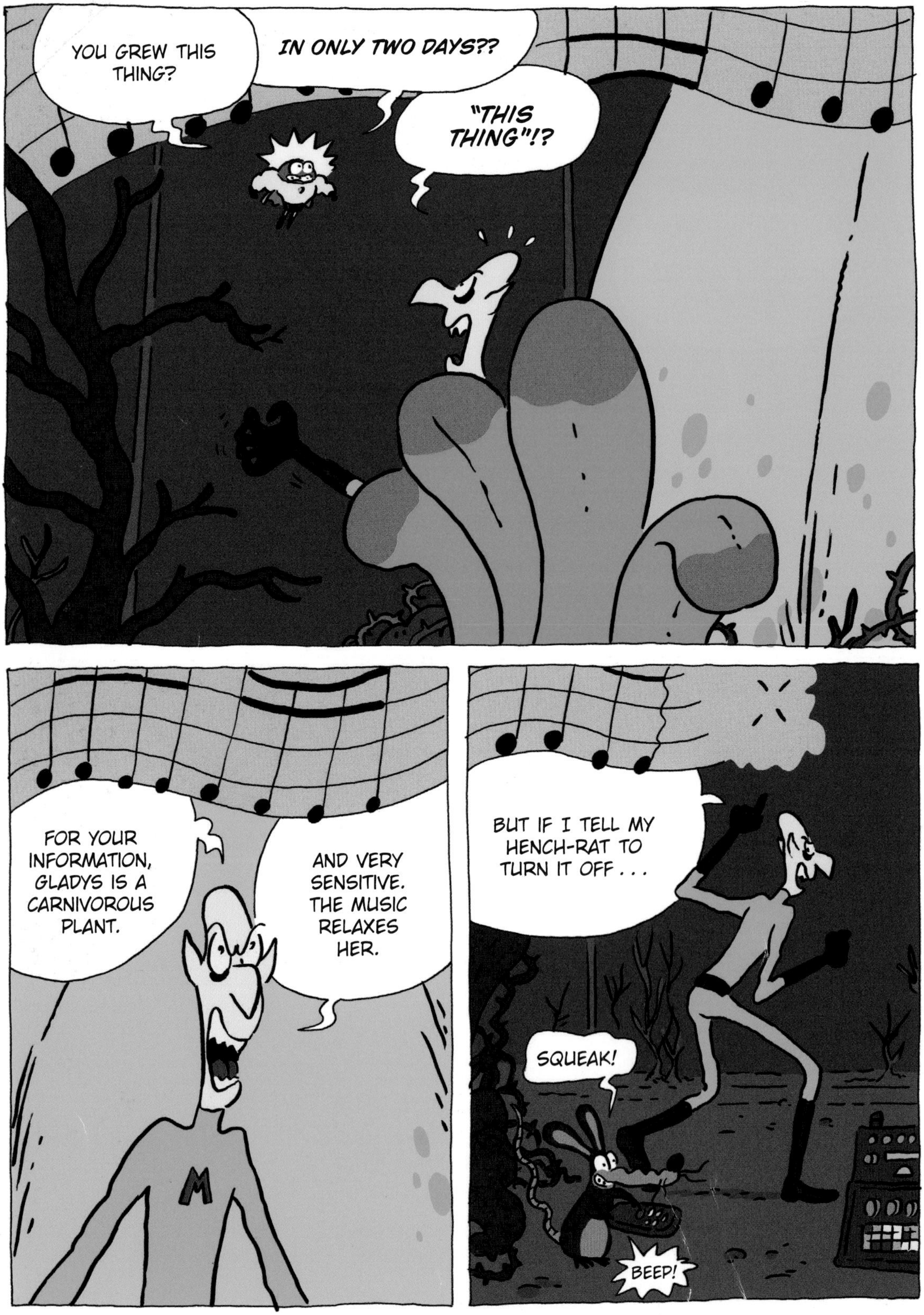
YOU GREW THIS THING?
IN ONLY TWO DAYS??
"THIS THING"!?
FOR YOUR INFORMATION, GLADYS IS A CARNIVOROUS PLANT.
AND VERY SENSITIVE. THE MUSIC RELAXES HER.
BUT IF I TELL MY HENCH-RAT TO TURN IT OFF . . .
SQUEAK!
BEEP!

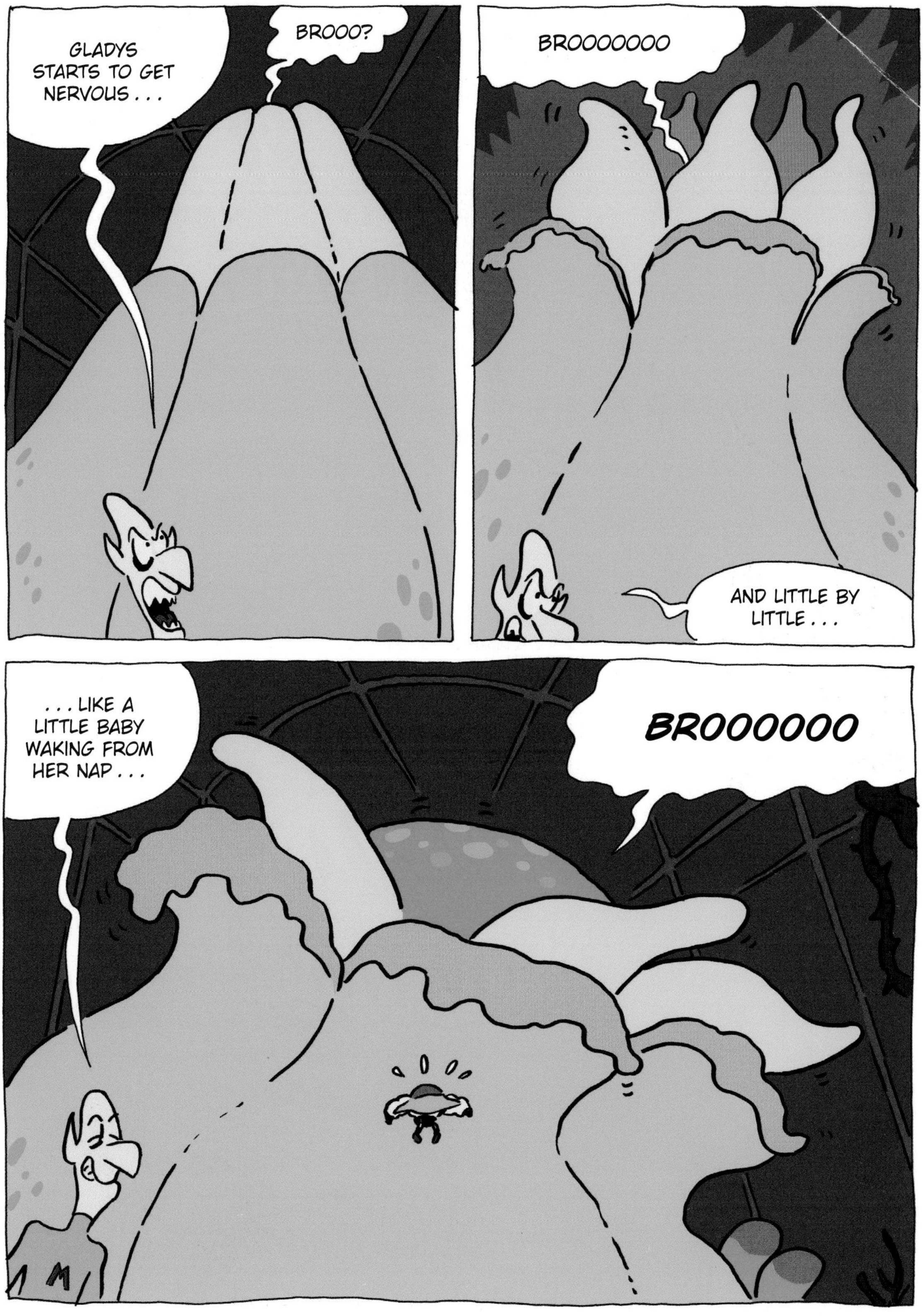
GLADYS STARTS TO GET NERVOUS . . .
BROOO?
BROOOOOOO
AND LITTLE BY LITTLE . . .
. . . LIKE A LITTLE BABY WAKING FROM HER NAP . . .
BROOOOOO

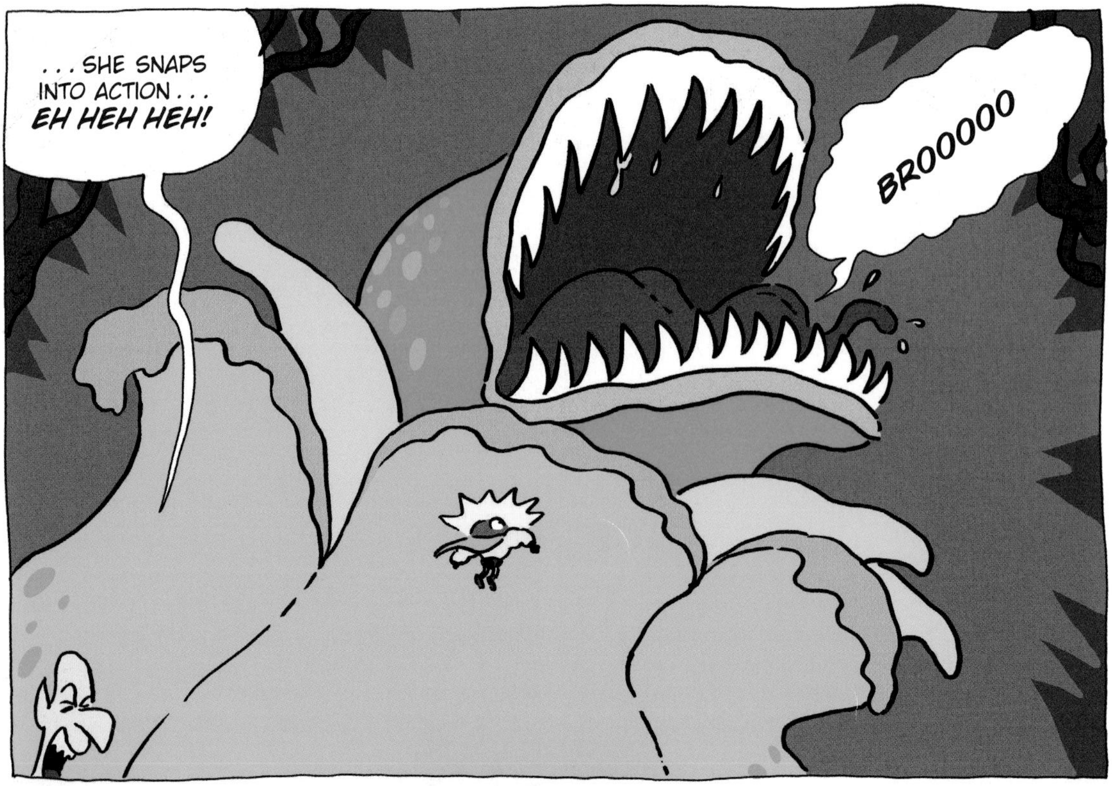

. . . SHE SNAPS INTO ACTION . . . EH HEH HEH!
BROOOOO

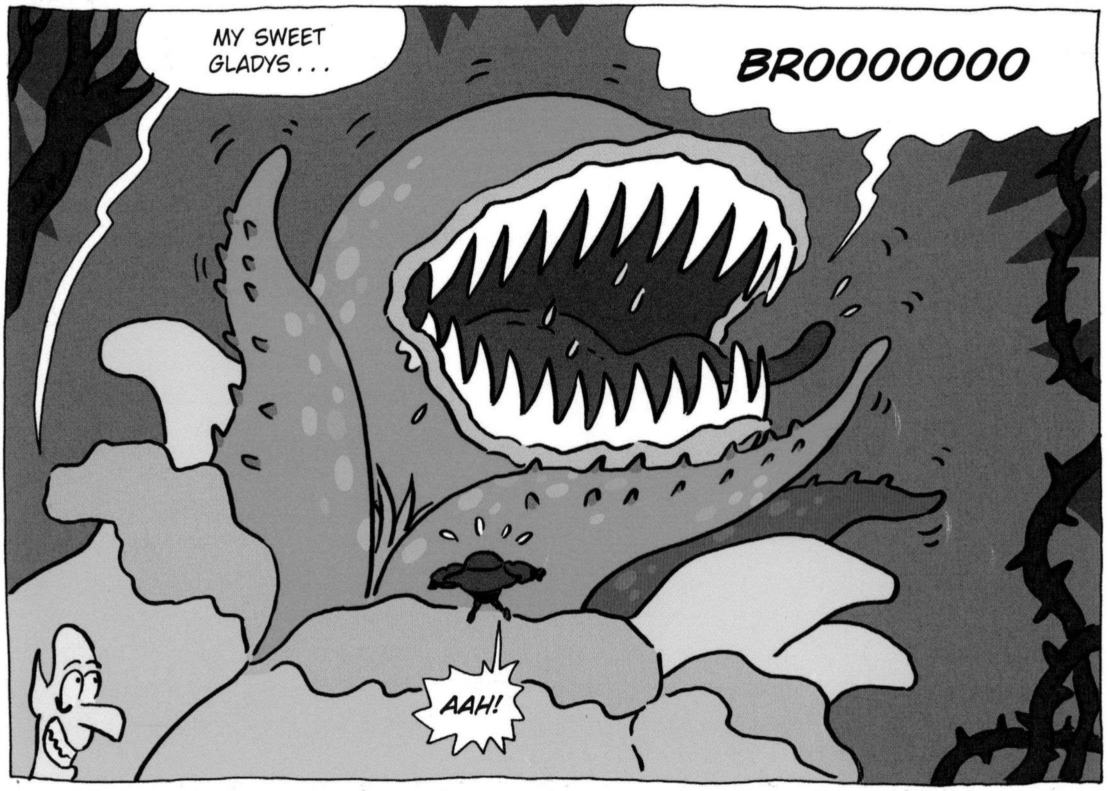

MY SWEET GLADYS . . .
BROOOOOOO
AAH!

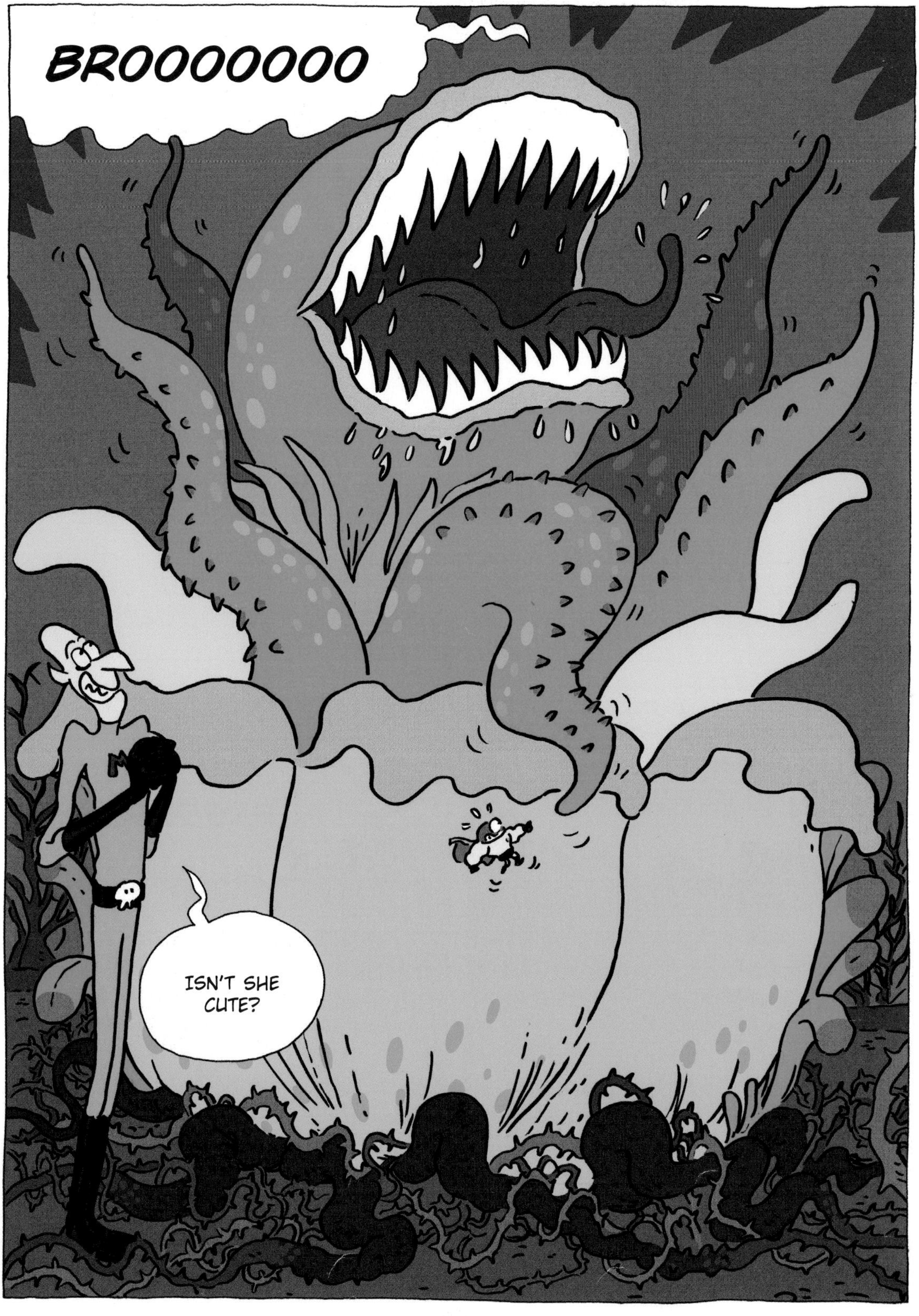
BROOOOOOO
ISN'T SHE CUTE?

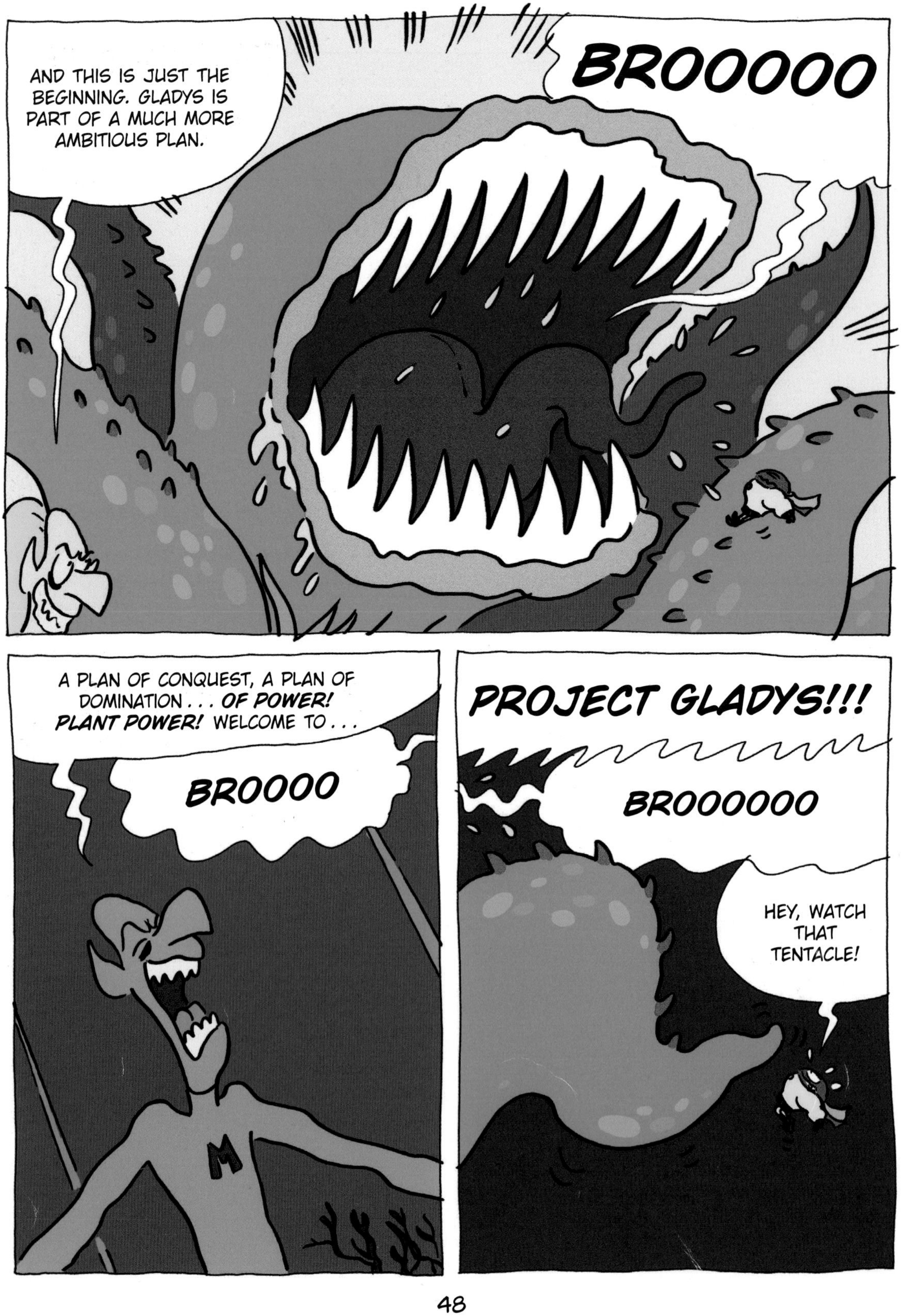
AND THIS IS JUST THE BEGINNING. GLADYS IS PART OF A MUCH MORE AMBITIOUS PLAN.
BROOOOO
A PLAN OF CONQUEST, A PLAN OF DOMINATION . . . *OF POWER! PLANT POWER!* WELCOME TO . . .
BROOOO
PROJECT GLADYS!!!
BROOOOOO
HEY, WATCH THAT TENTACLE!

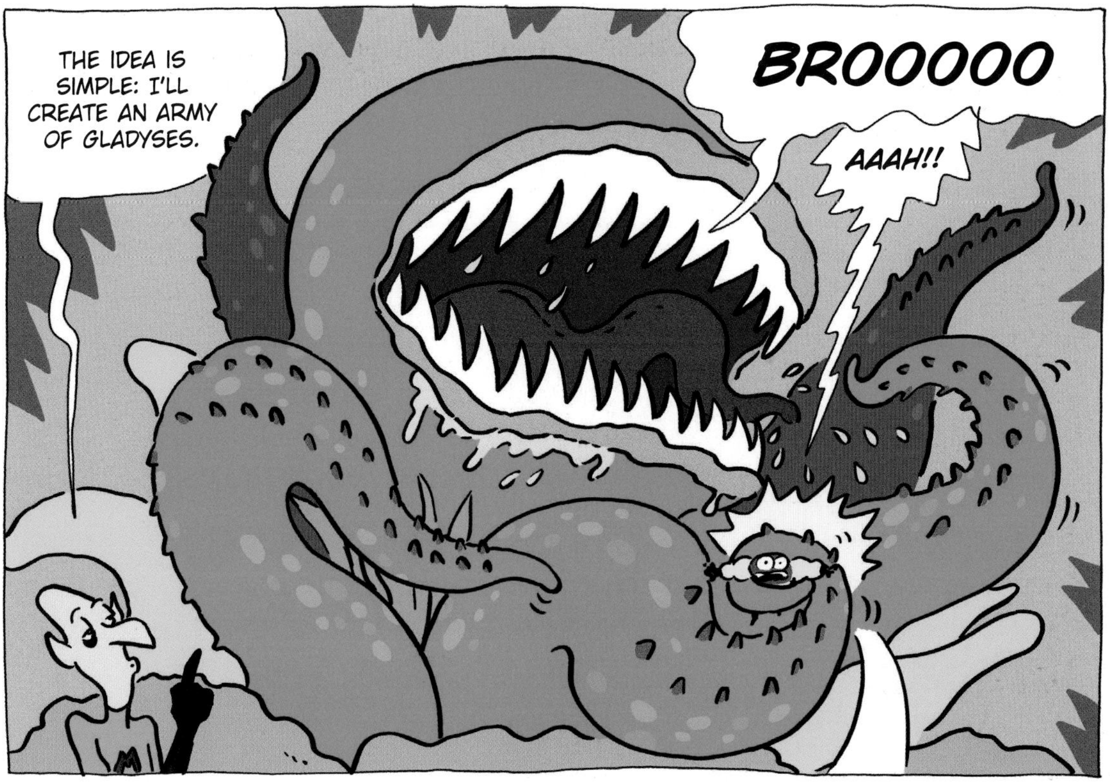
THE IDEA IS SIMPLE: I'LL CREATE AN ARMY OF GLADYSES.
BROOOOO
AAAH!!

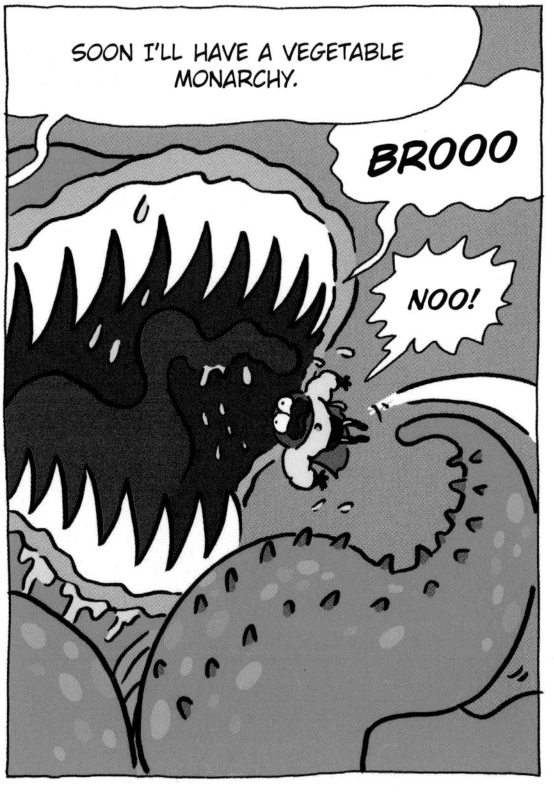
SOON I'LL HAVE A VEGETABLE MONARCHY.
BROOO
NOO!

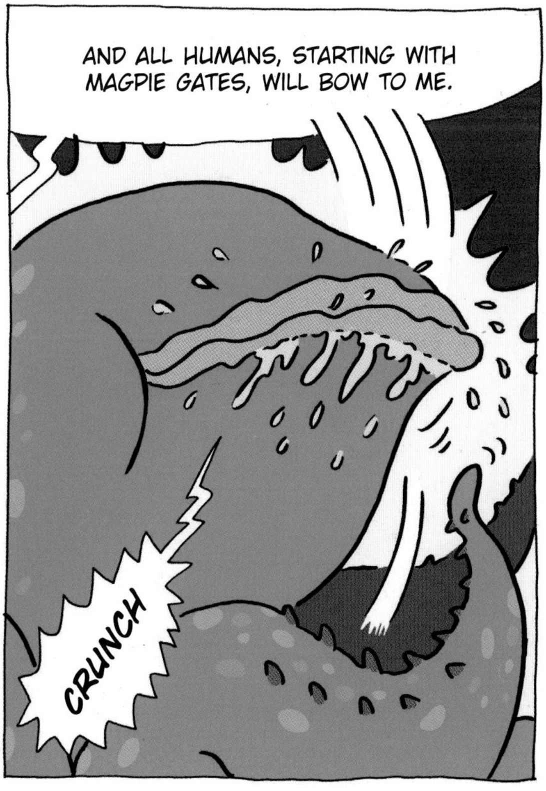
AND ALL HUMANS, STARTING WITH MAGPIE GATES, WILL BOW TO ME.
CRUNCH

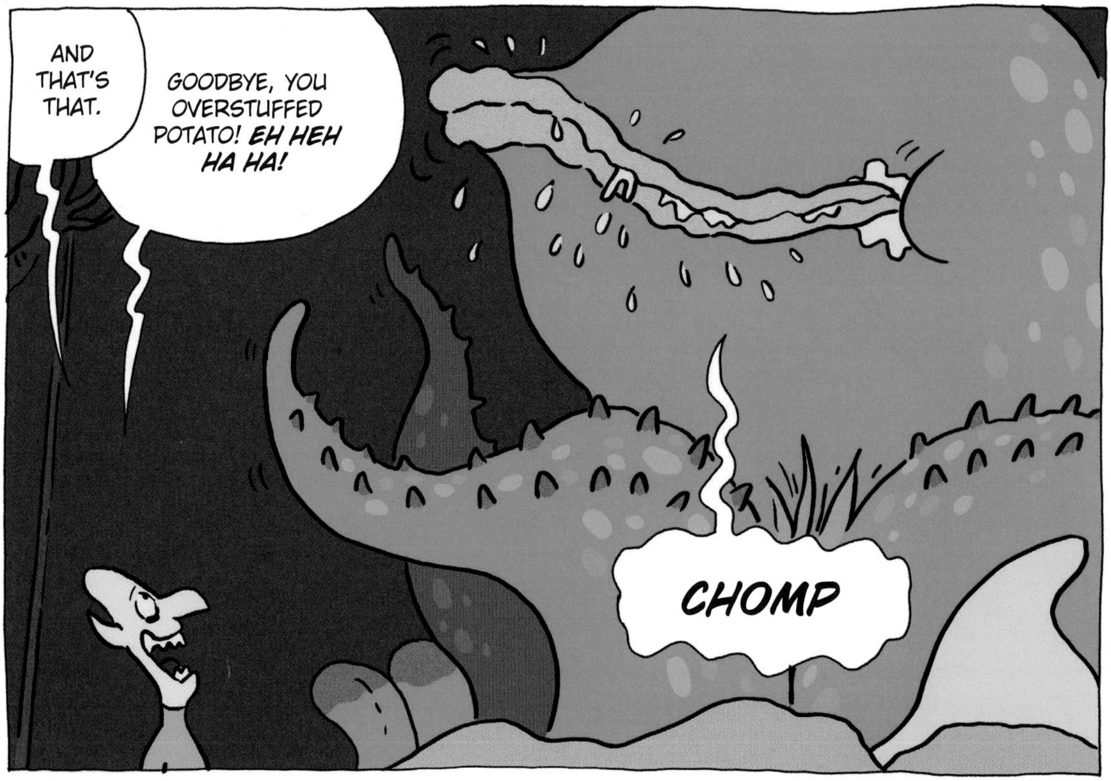
AND THAT'S THAT.
GOODBYE, YOU OVERSTUFFED POTATO! **EH HEH HA HA!**
CHOMP

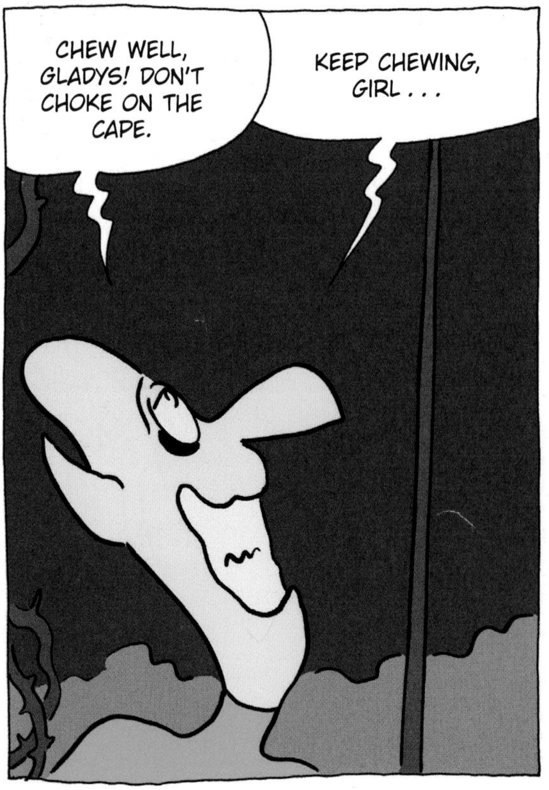
CHEW WELL, GLADYS! DON'T CHOKE ON THE CAPE.
KEEP CHEWING, GIRL . . .

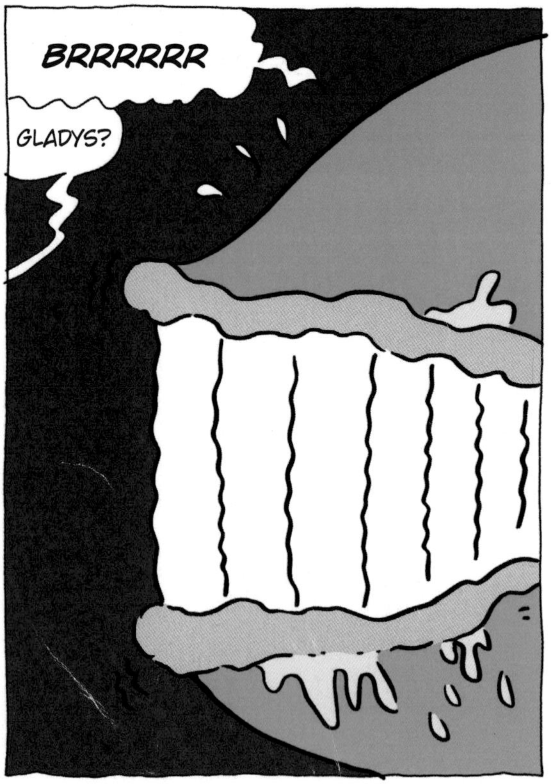
BRRRRRR
GLADYS?

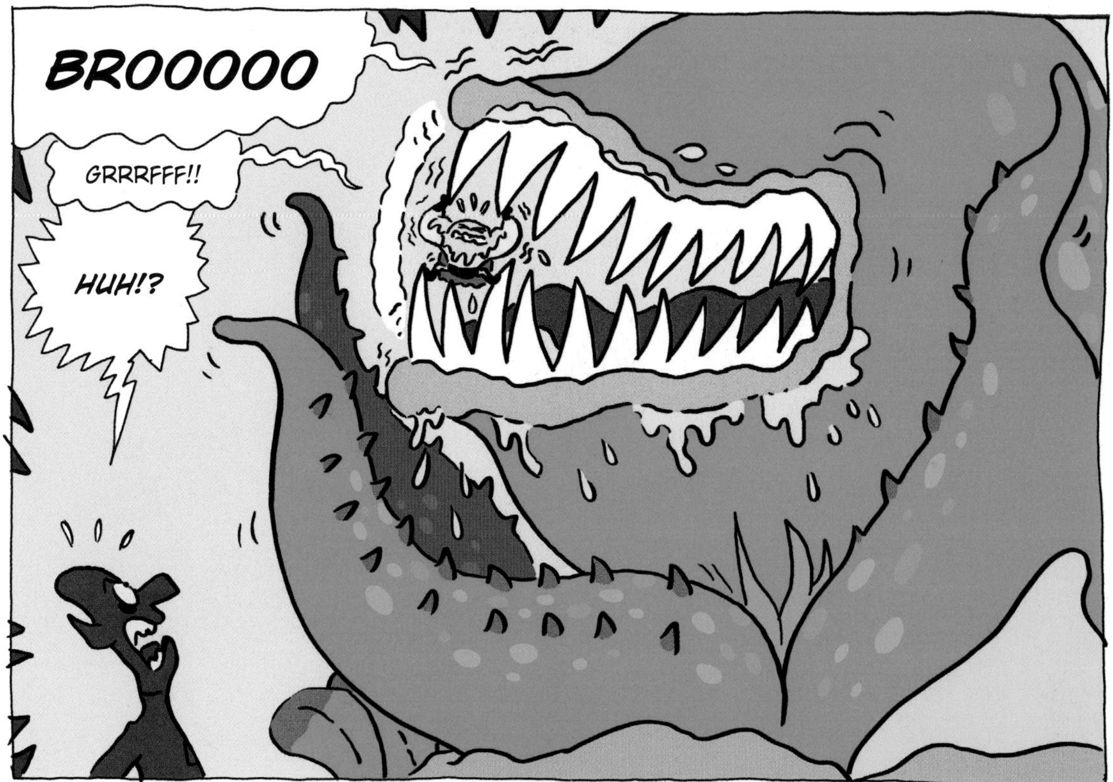
BROOOOO
GRRRFFF!!
HUH!?

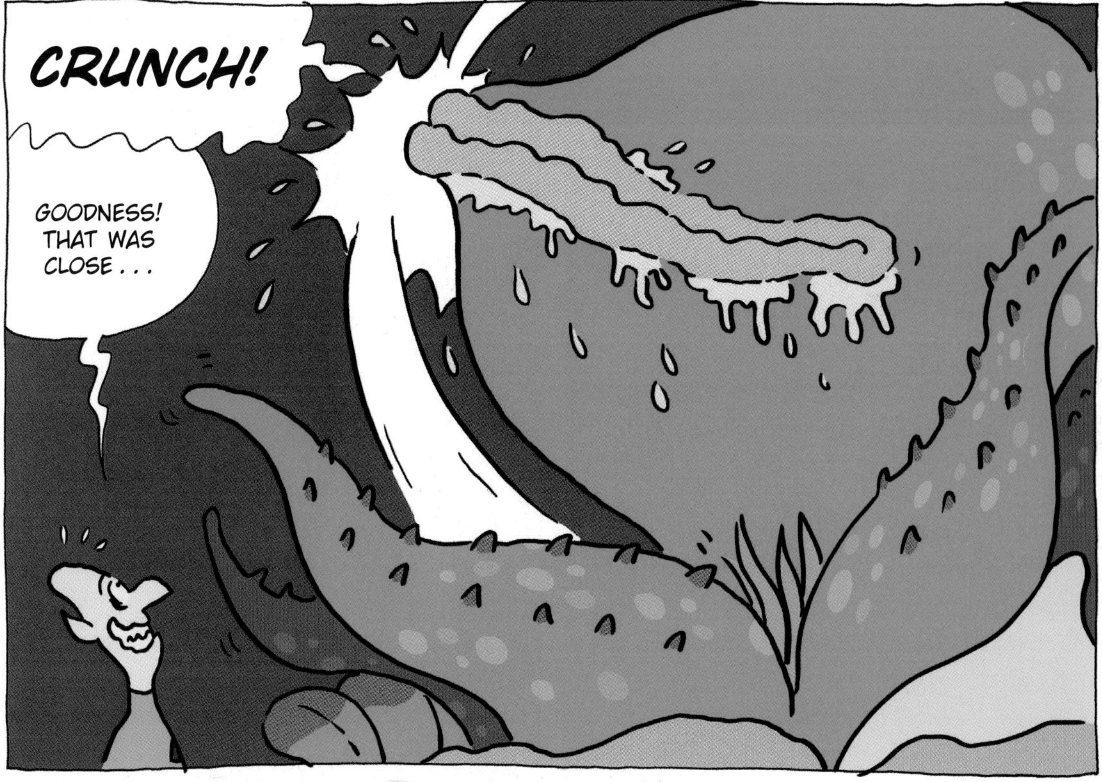
CRUNCH!
GOODNESS! THAT WAS CLOSE . . .

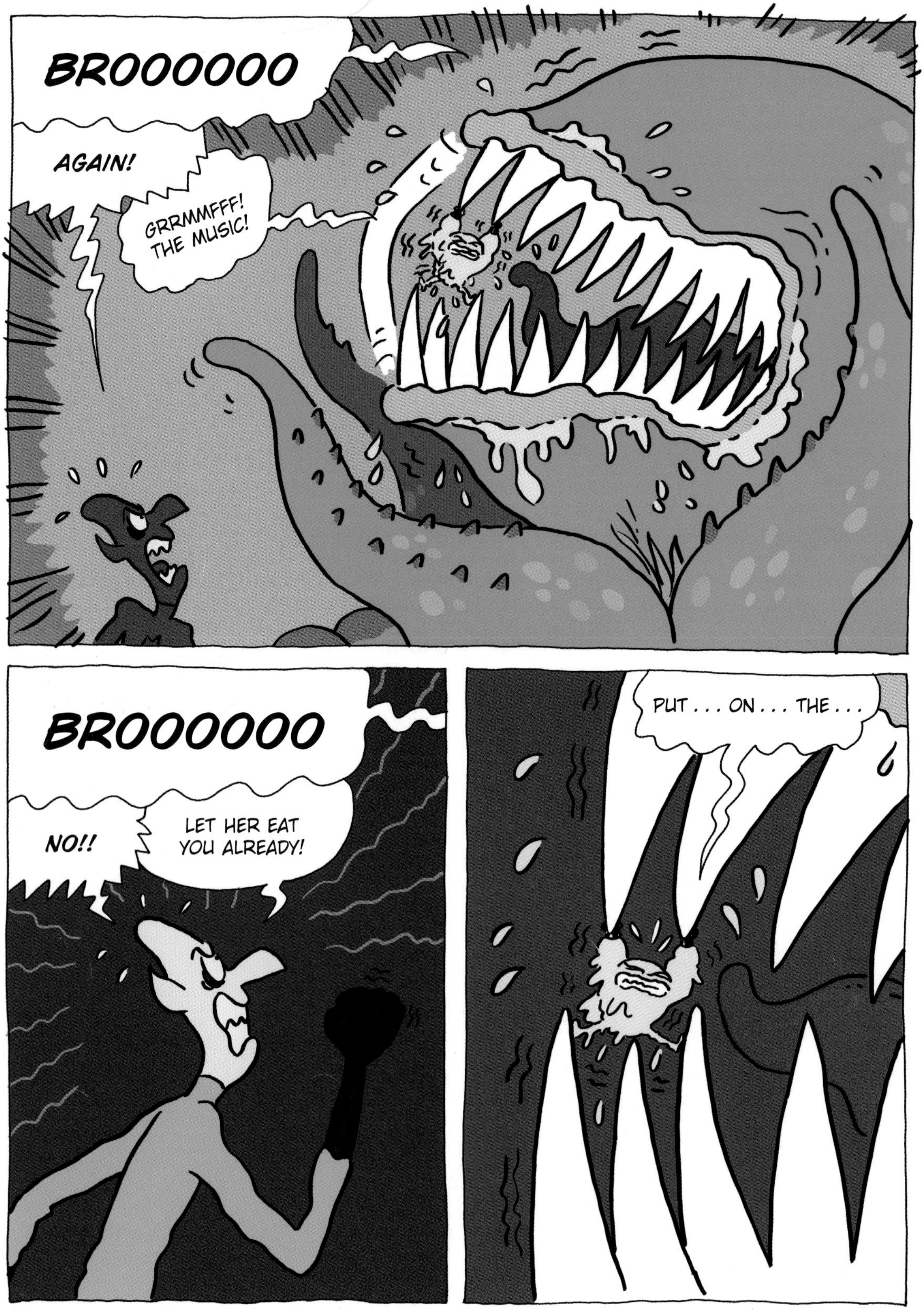
BROOOOOO
AGAIN!
GRRMMFFF! THE MUSIC!
BROOOOOO
NO!!
LET HER EAT YOU ALREADY!
PUT . . . ON . . . THE . . .

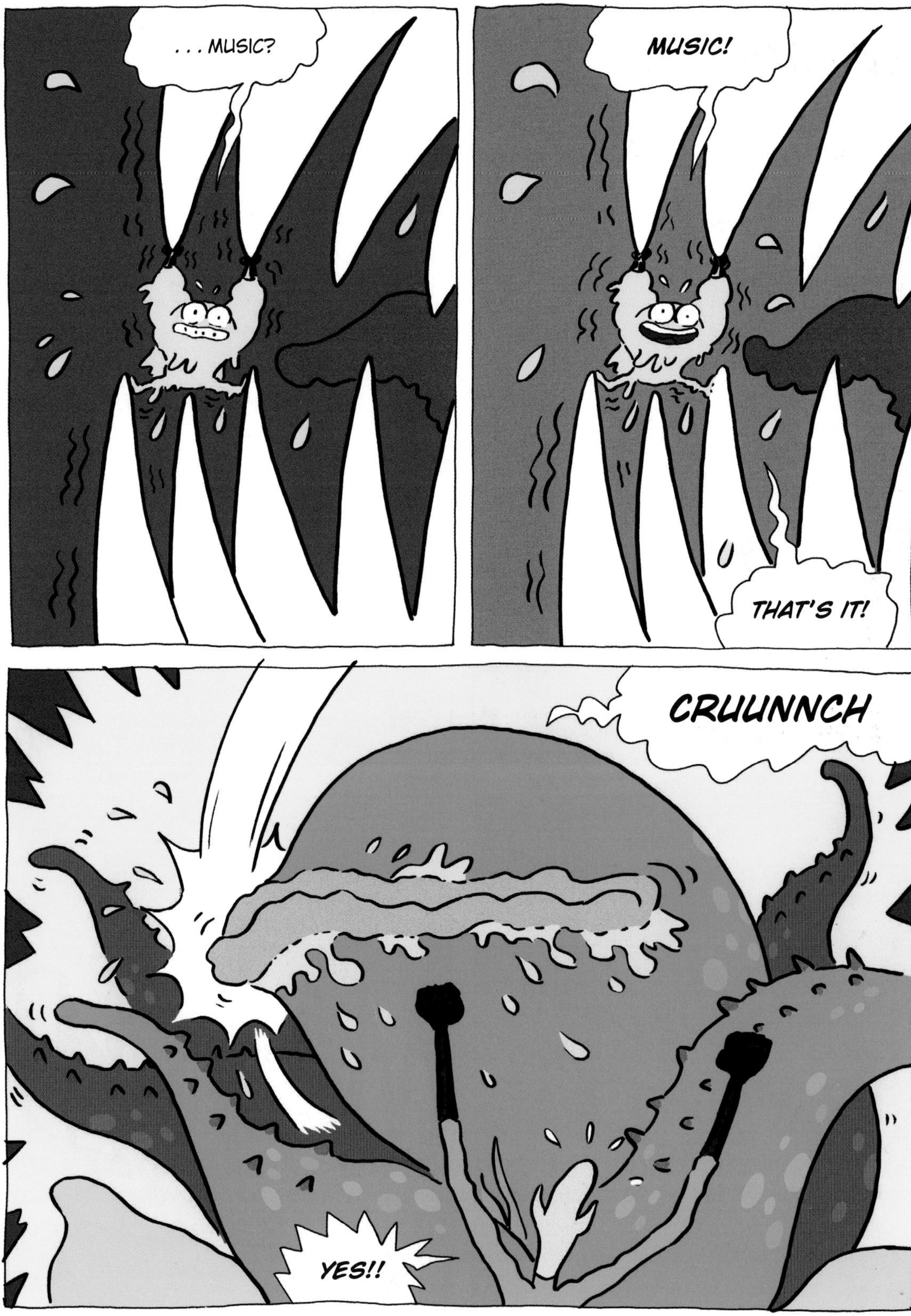

. . . MUSIC?
MUSIC!
THAT'S IT!
CRUUNNCH
YES!!

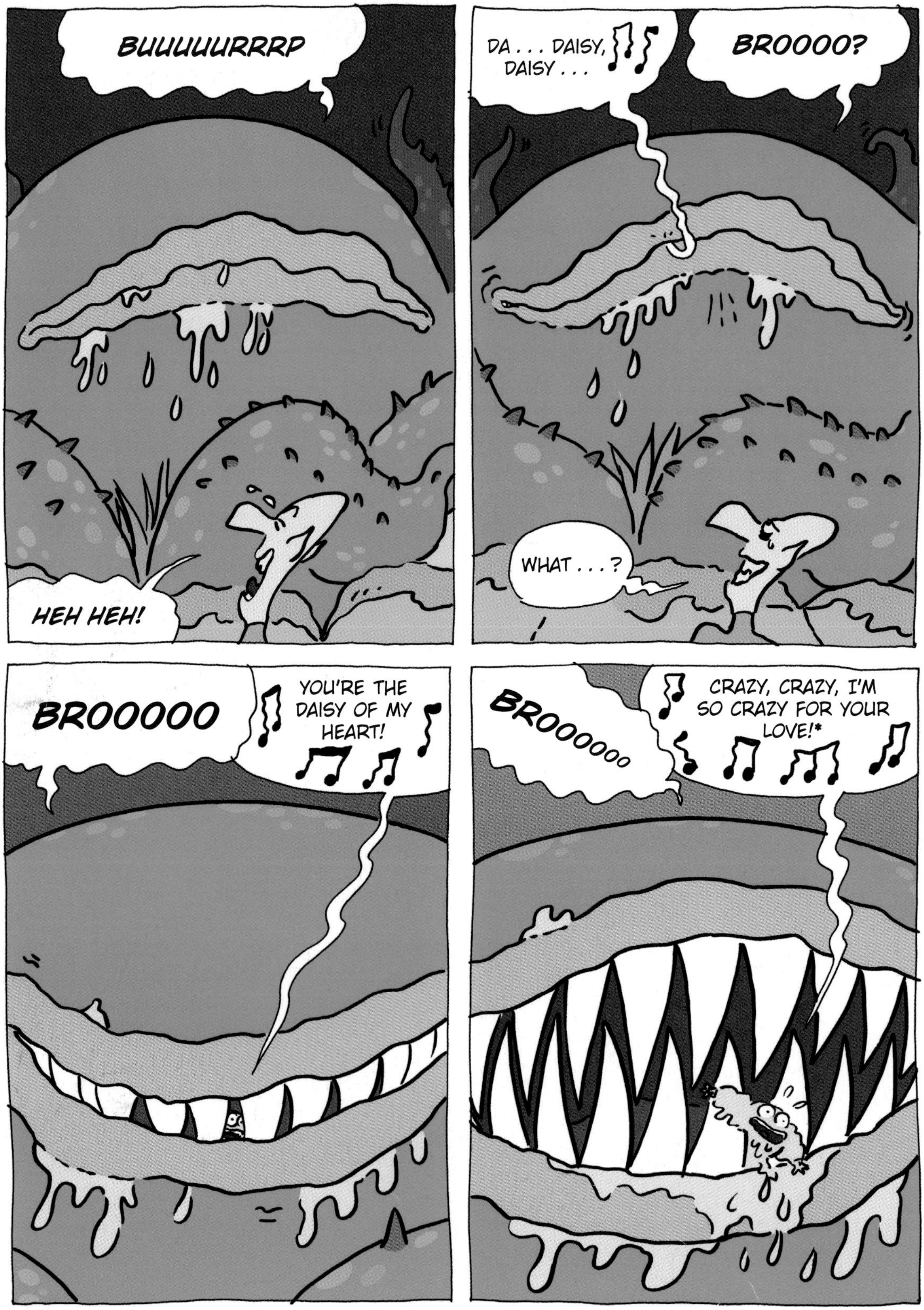
BUUUUURRRP
HEH HEH!
DA . . . DAISY, DAISY . . .
BROOOO?
WHAT . . . ?
BROOOOO
YOU'RE THE DAISY OF MY HEART!
BROOOOOOO
CRAZY, CRAZY, I'M SO CRAZY FOR YOUR LOVE!*

*THE HIT SONG FIRST HEARD IN
SUPER POTATO'S GALACTIC BREAKOUT

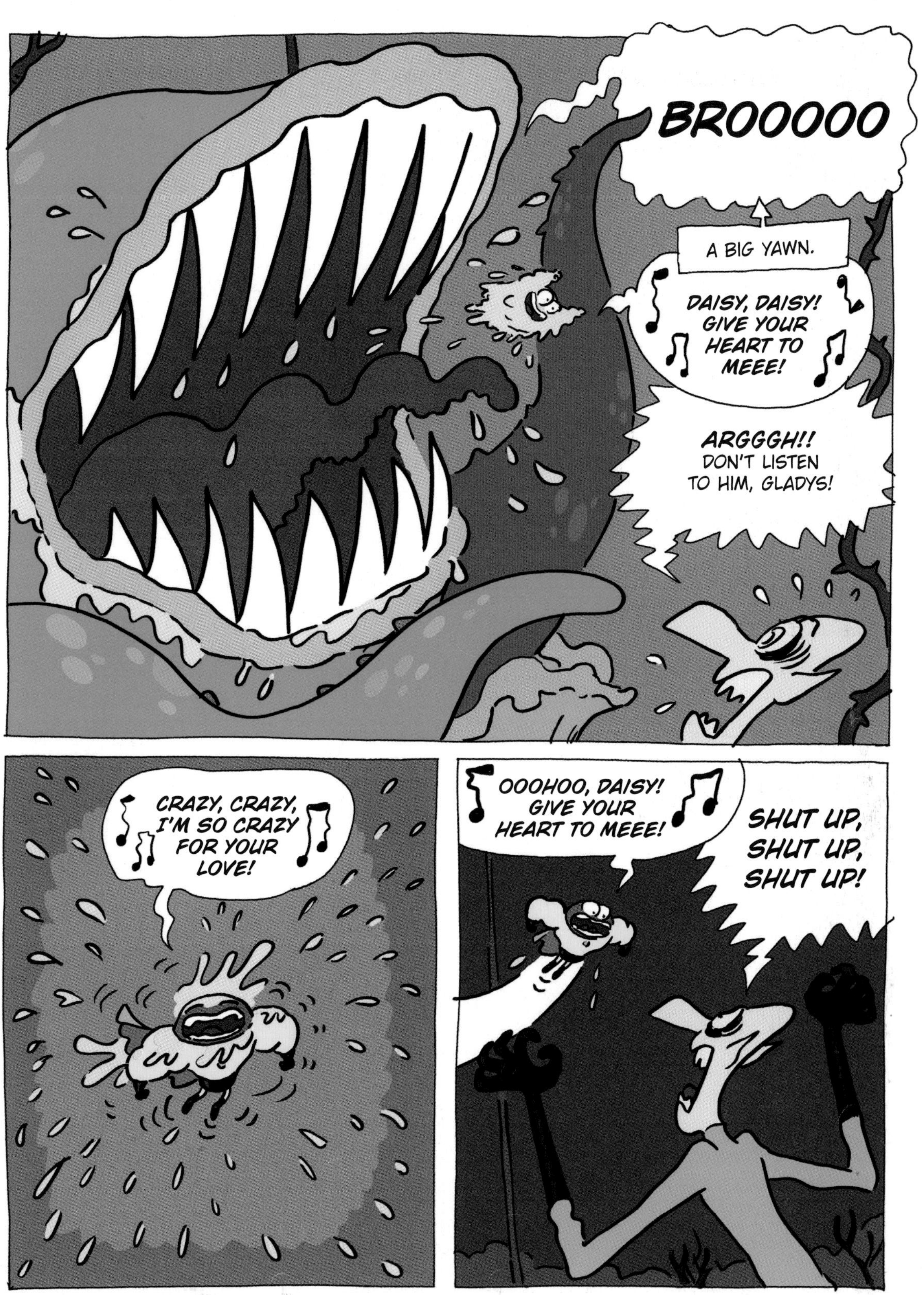
BROOOOO
A BIG YAWN.
DAISY, DAISY! GIVE YOUR HEART TO MEEE!
ARGGGH!! DON'T LISTEN TO HIM, GLADYS!
CRAZY, CRAZY, I'M SO CRAZY FOR YOUR LOVE!
OOOHOO, DAISY! GIVE YOUR HEART TO MEEE!
SHUT UP, SHUT UP, SHUT UP!

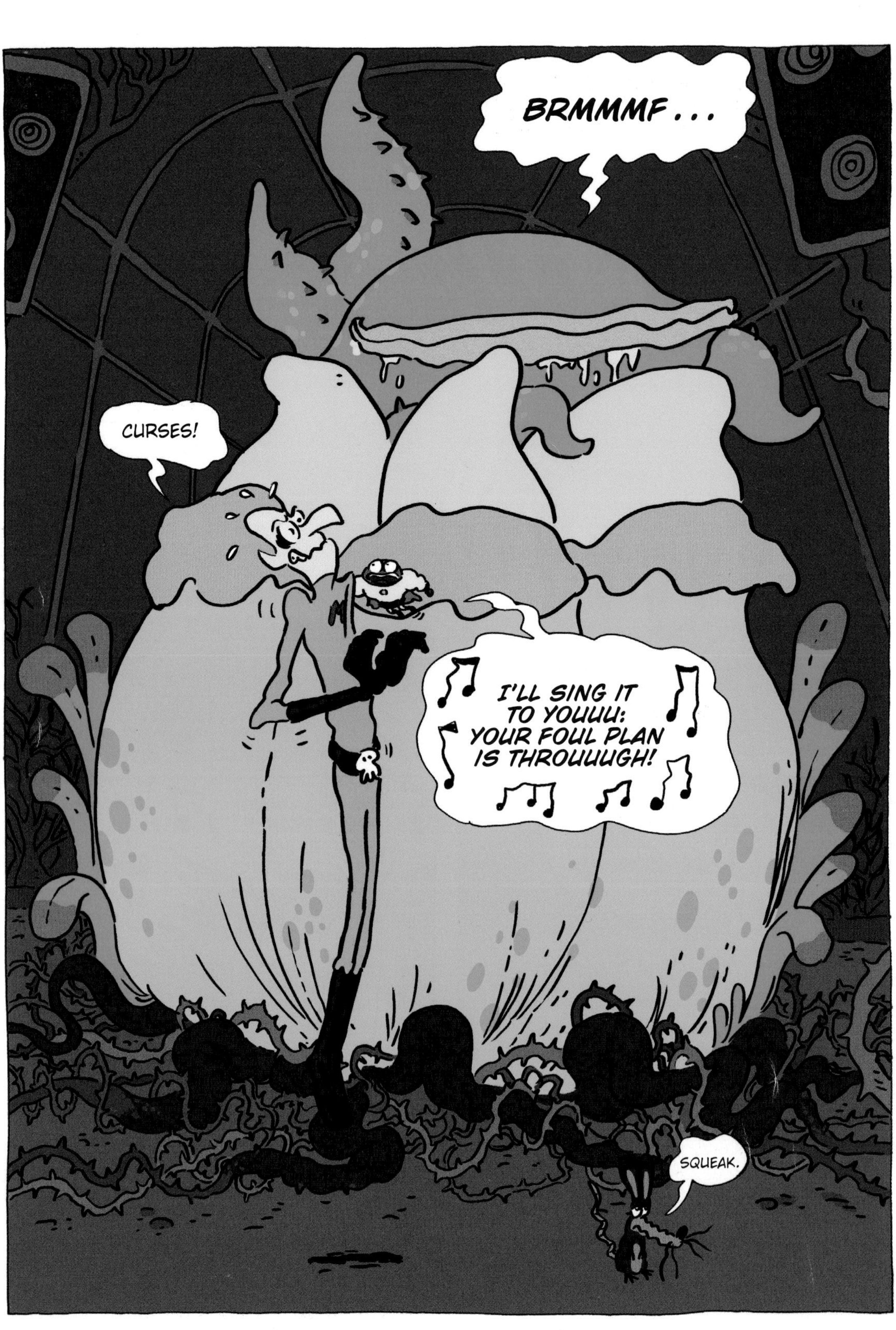
BRMMMF . . .
CURSES!
I'LL SING IT TO YOUUU: YOUR FOUL PLAN IS THROUUUGH!
SQUEAK.

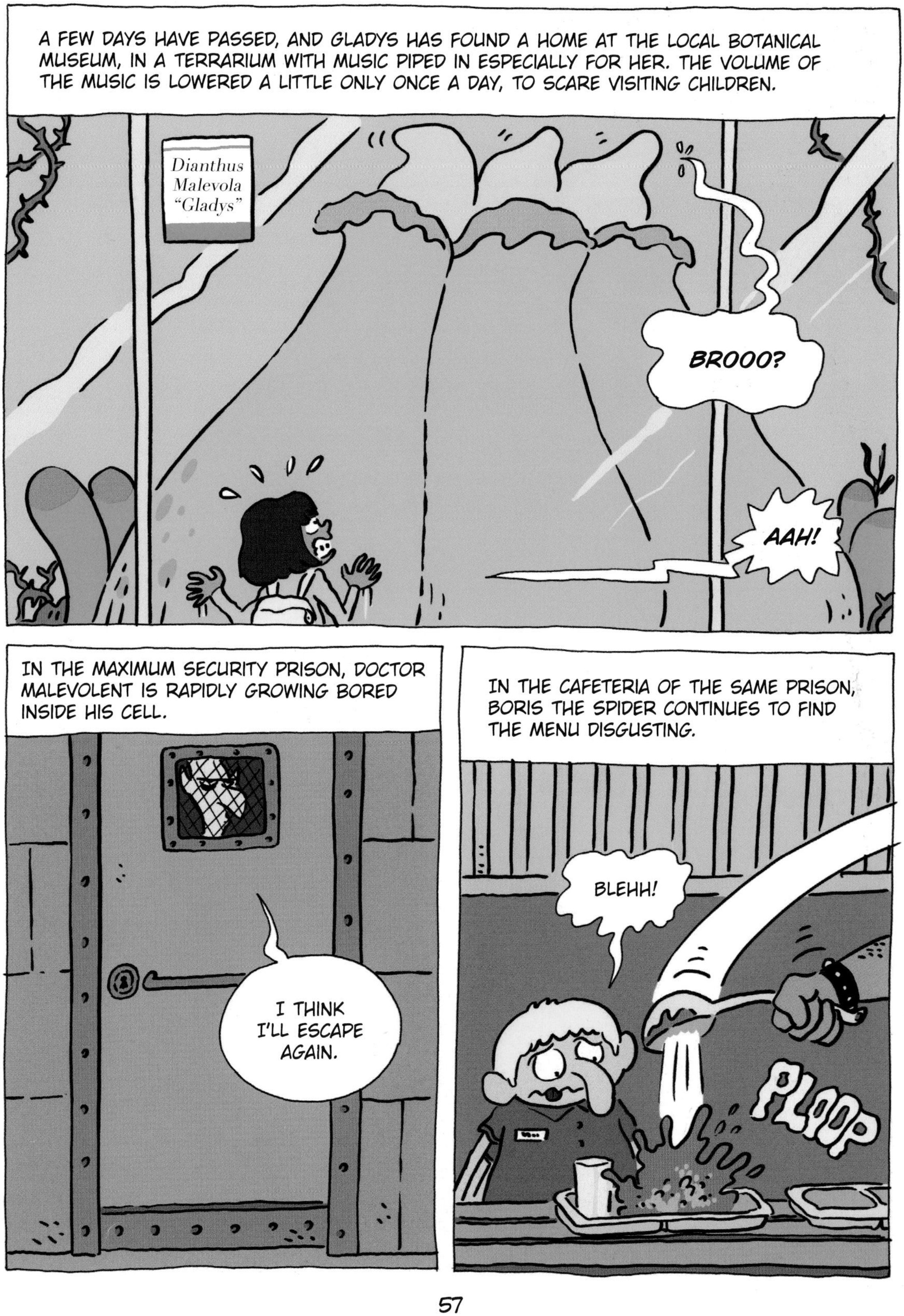
A FEW DAYS HAVE PASSED, AND GLADYS HAS FOUND A HOME AT THE LOCAL BOTANICAL MUSEUM, IN A TERRARIUM WITH MUSIC PIPED IN ESPECIALLY FOR HER. THE VOLUME OF THE MUSIC IS LOWERED A LITTLE ONLY ONCE A DAY, TO SCARE VISITING CHILDREN.
Dianthus Malevola "Gladys"
BROOO?
AAH!
IN THE MAXIMUM SECURITY PRISON, DOCTOR MALEVOLENT IS RAPIDLY GROWING BORED INSIDE HIS CELL.
I THINK I'LL ESCAPE AGAIN.
IN THE CAFETERIA OF THE SAME PRISON, BORIS THE SPIDER CONTINUES TO FIND THE MENU DISGUSTING.
BLEHH!
PLOOP

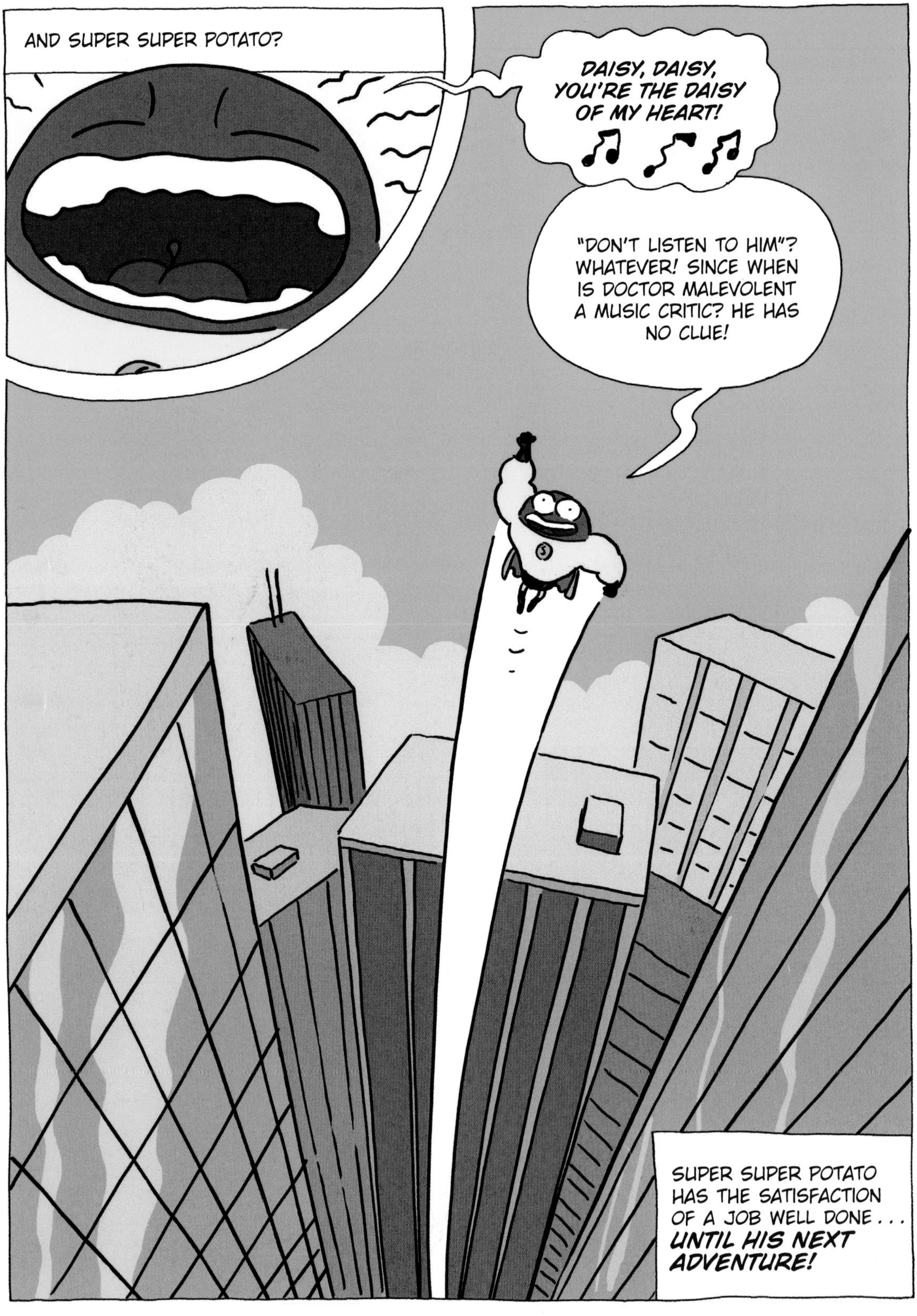
AND SUPER SUPER POTATO?
DAISY, DAISY, YOU'RE THE DAISY OF MY HEART!
"DON'T LISTEN TO HIM"? WHATEVER! SINCE WHEN IS DOCTOR MALEVOLENT A MUSIC CRITIC? HE HAS NO CLUE!
SUPER SUPER POTATO HAS THE SATISFACTION OF A JOB WELL DONE . . . UNTIL HIS NEXT ADVENTURE!

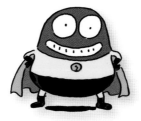

For more hilarious tales of Super Potato, check out . . .

SUPER POTATO
#1 THE EPIC ORIGIN OF SUPER POTATO
Artur Laperla

SUPER POTATO
#2 SUPER POTATO'S GALACTIC BREAKOUT
Artur Laperla

SUPER POTATO
#3 SUPER POTATO'S MEGA TIME-TRAVEL ADVENTURE

SUPER POTATO
#4 SUPER POTATO AND THE MUTANT ANIMAL MAYHEM
Artur Laperla

SUPER POTATO
#5 SUPER POTATO AND THE CASTLE OF ROBOTS
Artur Laperla

SUPER POTATO
#6 SUPER POTATO GETS BUFF

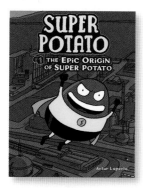

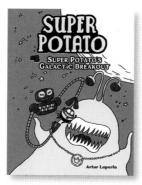

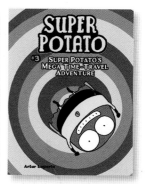

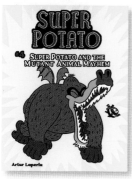

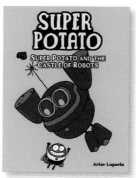

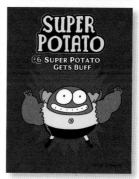

AND TURN THE PAGE FOR A PREVIEW OF OUR HERO'S NEXT GREAT ADVENTURE . . .

SUPER POTATO #8

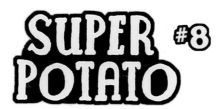

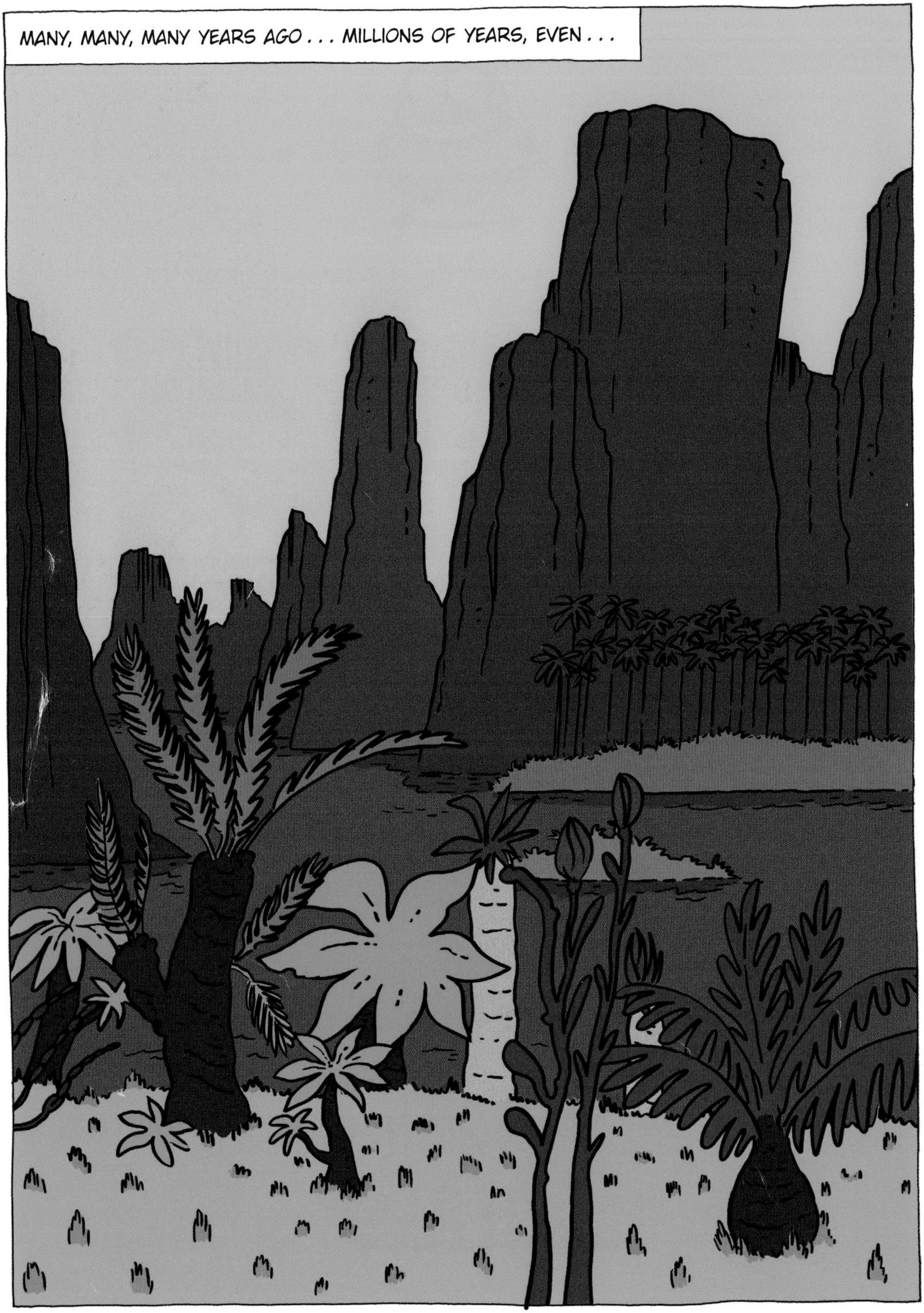
MANY, MANY, MANY YEARS AGO . . . MILLIONS OF YEARS, EVEN . . .

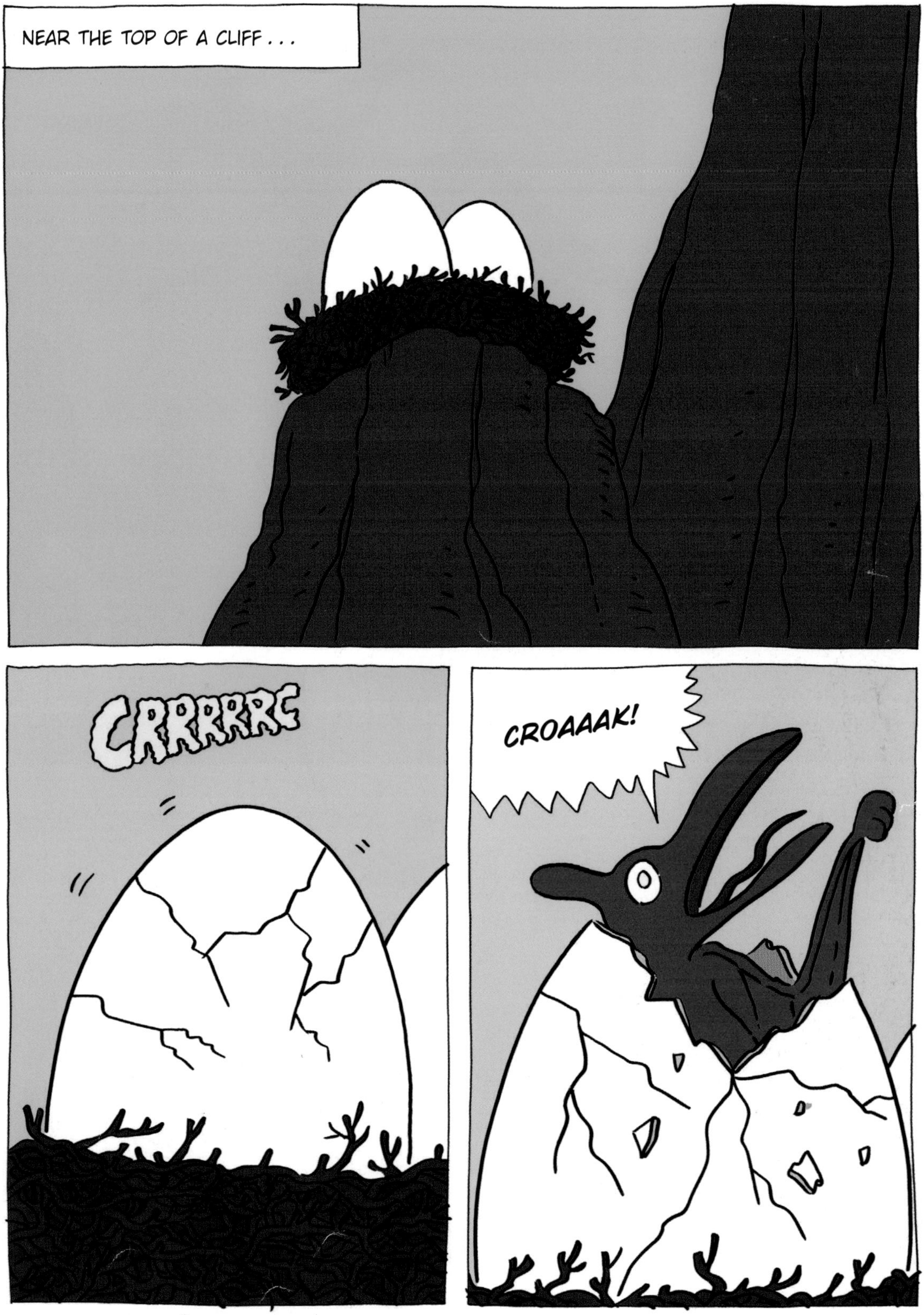
NEAR THE TOP OF A CLIFF . . .
CRRRRRC
CROAAAK!

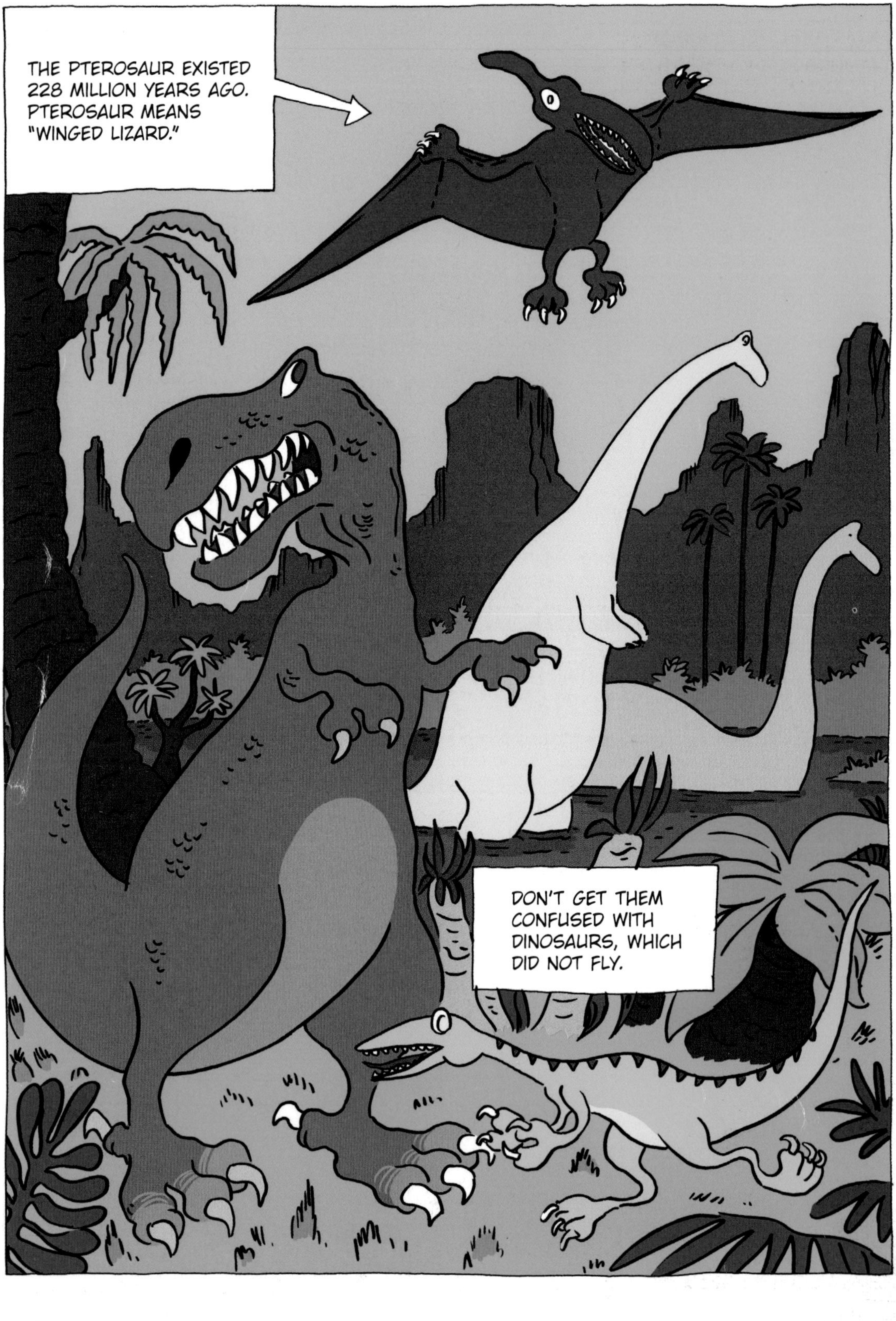
THE PTEROSAUR EXISTED 228 MILLION YEARS AGO. PTEROSAUR MEANS "WINGED LIZARD."
DON'T GET THEM CONFUSED WITH DINOSAURS, WHICH DID NOT FLY.

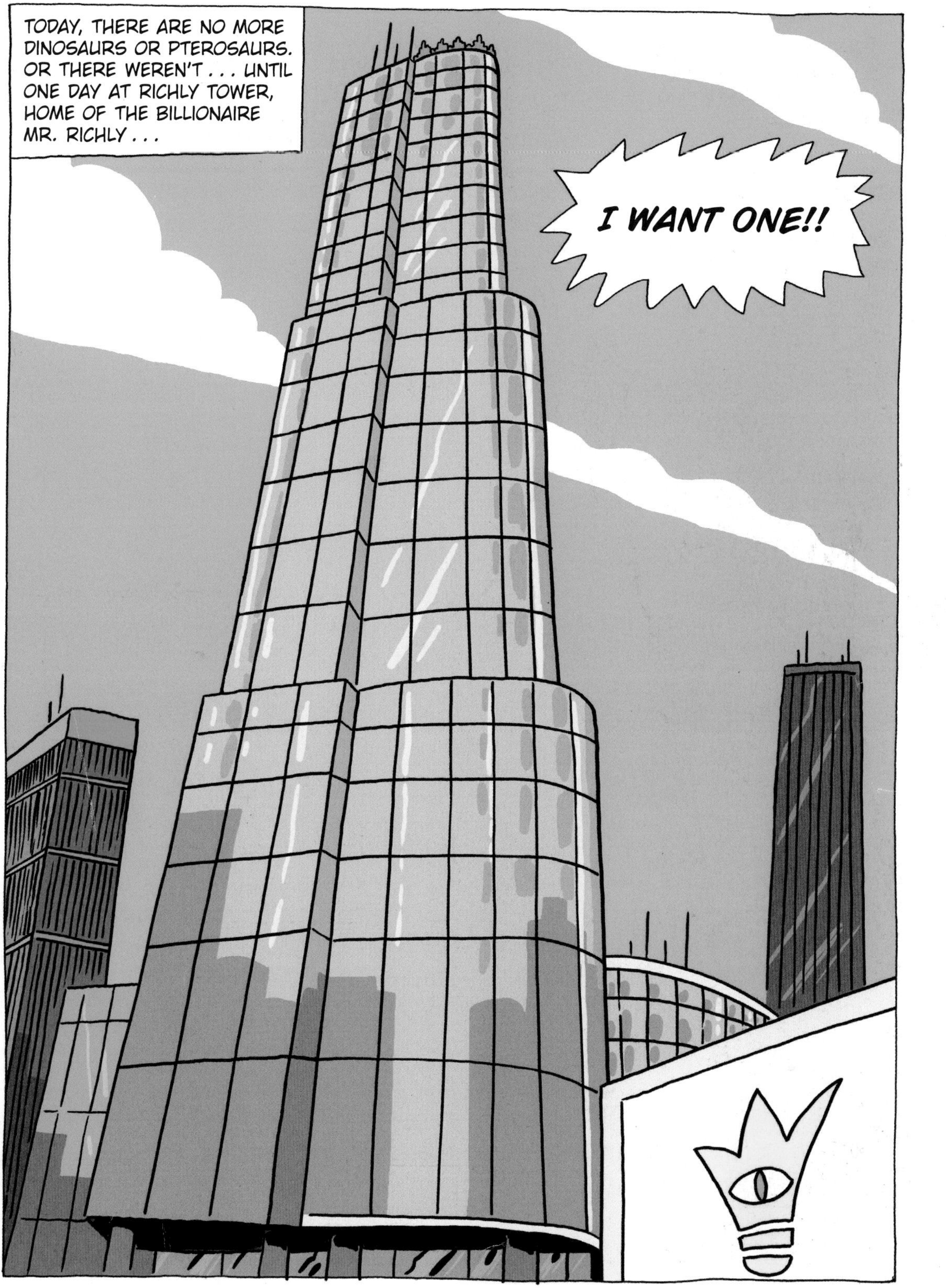
TODAY, THERE ARE NO MORE DINOSAURS OR PTEROSAURS. OR THERE WEREN'T . . . UNTIL ONE DAY AT RICHLY TOWER, HOME OF THE BILLIONAIRE MR. RICHLY . . .
I WANT ONE!!

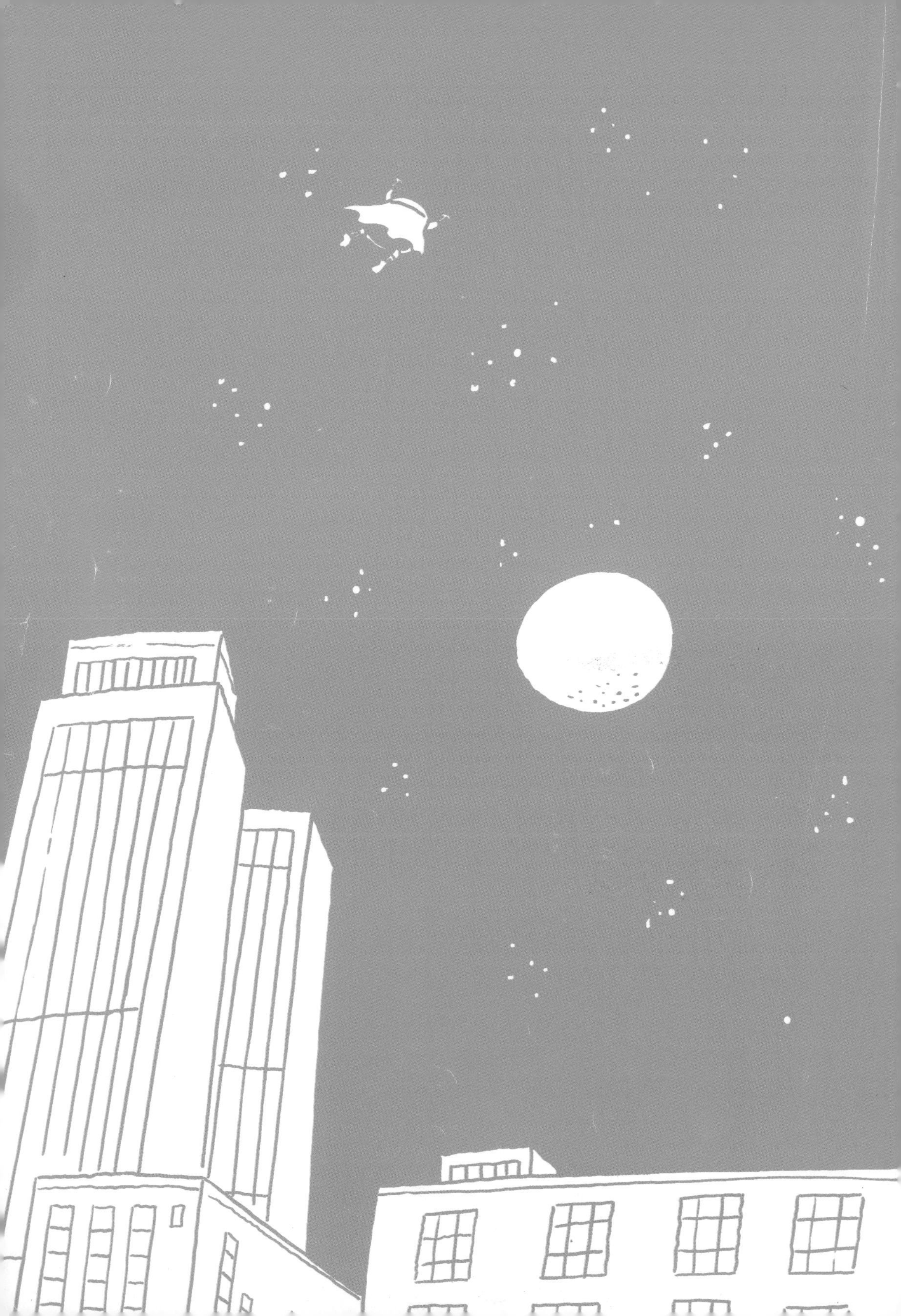